The Fabulous Mums of Champion Valley

Also by Zarreen Khan

Koi Good News?
My Best Friend's Son's Wedding

The Fabulous Mums of Champion Valley

ZARREEN KHAN

First published in India by Harper Fiction 2024
An imprint of HarperCollins *Publishers*
4th Floor, Tower A, Building No. 10, Phase II, DLF Cyber City,
Gurugram, Haryana – 122002
www.harpercollins.co.in

2 4 6 8 10 9 7 5 3 1

Copyright © Zarreen Khan 2024

P-ISBN: 978-93-6213-561-2
E-ISBN: 978-93-6213-837-8

This is a work of fiction and all characters and incidents described in this book are the product of the author's imagination. Any resemblance to actual persons, living or dead, is entirely coincidental.

Zarreen Khan asserts the moral right
to be identified as the author of this work.

All rights reserved. No part of this publication may be reproduced, stored in a retrieval system, or transmitted, in any form or by any means, electronic, mechanical, photocopying, recording or otherwise, without the prior permission of the publishers.

Typeset in 10.5/13.5 Sabon LT Std at
Manipal Technologies Limited, Manipal

Printed and bound at
Replika Press Pvt. Ltd.

This book is produced from independently certified FSC® paper to ensure responsible forest management.

*To all the mums out there,
who keep the show running
even if it's on Comedy Central*

From: The Desk of the Principal
Champion Valley School
Golf Links Estate
Gurugram
Haryana, 122002

18 February 2022

<u>Sub: Appointment Letter</u>

Dear Ms Ambika S.,

It gives me great pleasure to welcome you onboard as a full-time faculty member at Champion Valley School. You have been appointed as Class Teacher, Grade III, for the Academic Year 2022–23.

It is our constant endeavour to include individuals in the Champion Valley family, who are passionate and committed towards building an education ecosystem in line with our core values—Integrity, Perseverance and Consciousness. We want our students to become flagbearers of free thought, and, as an educator, your role is critical in shaping their future. May we all succeed in our pursuit of excellence across all fields—academic as well as non-academic.

The details of your employment are attached herewith. Kindly send us a signed acceptance of the same.

Regards,

Malini M.

Malini Mehta
Principal, Champion Valley School

Ambika

It was as if someone had eaten a thesaurus for breakfast and spewed out this splattering of words—loosely resembling sentences—on a piece of paper. 'Pursuit of excellence'. 'Flagbearers of free thought'. 'Education ecosystem'. 'Integrity, perseverance and ...', wait for it, 'consciousness'! What did that even mean? Was it a school for zombies? Did the students come to school in comatose condition?

It established its authority by using unnecessarily complicated jargon, even if its primary stakeholders were uneducated five-year-olds. Even I, aged thirty, had to read that letter three times to make sense of it. What exactly was being asked of me? To shape their future? Sure, if amoeba is counted as a shape. Because that was the shape of my own life now. Fluid and directionless. Meandering and ambiguous. Confused. Not to forget, pretty much asexual of late.

But I knew I was being ungrateful. This was a skill I was most competent in. I had a gratitude journal lying by my bedside, waiting to be inaugurated, and this offer letter would have been a great way to get started—but I was, instead, viewing the letter with absolute contempt. Spend eight hours of my day surrounded by snotty little monsters voluntarily? No, thank you!

Of course, I knew what a great opportunity it was. Parents fought bloody wars to get their children admitted to CVS, and many embarked on pilgrimages to give thanks once they were successful. I had seen stickers on cars that read 'Proud CVS Mom', 'CVS Dads', 'There is no such thing as perfect parenting, but my kid goes to CVS', and so on. Like, calm down! It's only a school!

The only thing my own school could ever claim was: 'Convent girls in short skirts, can kick you where it really hurts'. But then the education system had undergone quite a transformation over the years, as my best friend Dodo told me. Teachers were now kinder, academics were experiential, marks weren't the only measure of learning, overall development in children was encouraged and parents suddenly seemed to be far more involved with their children and actually believed that the power of words worked better than the power of chappal.

Yet, that doubt nagged me. Was I really doing this? Was I choosing this life?

Was I *choosing* to be surrounded by tiny human beings that I didn't give birth to? Was I choosing to wake up at the crack of dawn and board a yellow bus that would take me to an institution I'd often described as 'prison'? Was I being expected to discipline eight-year-olds when I'd spent most of my own schooling hours in detention? Was I being asked to hold them accountable for not doing their homework when my imaginary dog had perpetually feasted on mine? Was I being asked to maintain discipline and pin drop silence in the class when my legendary note-passing skills in school could put any social network to shame? Was I choosing to be an educator, a disciplinarian, a rule enforcer—voluntarily?

Unfortunately, the answer was 'yes'. Because I had bills to pay, things to buy and places to be. And no other job was going to give me six-week-off at a stretch, allowing me to indulge in my real passion—travel. I had twenty-seven stamps on my passport, a massive map of India on my wall filled with travel pins, souvenirs and magnets framed and mounted in my living room ... and, yet, I wanted more. Even if it meant slaving away half my life as a primary school teacher. So, with much reluctance—and forced gratitude—I found myself completing the joining formalities.

This resulted in me getting rocket-launched into a series of excruciatingly boring training sessions—something I hadn't accounted for. It was ironic that I had to *study* to *teach*. But I went through the whole regime as a committed foot soldier—soft skills training, subject training, conflict training, personality training, and so on. And just when I thought I was doing pretty well, as is tradition for me, I was summoned to the principal's office. Even before the term had started!

Memories flooded my mind, as I walked down the sterile, quiet corridors of the administration block. It was like a parallel universe of the chaos in the classrooms on the other side of the building. All schools felt the same. And, oh, the countless principal visits I'd made as a student for things I had and had not done! The 'had not' mostly included homework and the 'had' covered everything else. The prickly anticipation of what my punishment would be this time—whether Dad would be called again, whether I'd be grounded, whether I'd be let off with a stern warning only. I'd been so glad to leave those days behind me. Yet, here I was again—and life had come a full circle for me. Even if it was, for a change, not as an errant student but as an 'empowered' teacher, as we had been defined in our 'Proud to Teach' training module.

I reached the end of the hallway and entered the brightly lit, freakishly clean glass cabin that bristled with the fragrance of an Elizabeth Arden perfume. My new employer indicated that I should take a seat and so I did, obediently. She really radiated authority. And she always had, Mrs Mehta, my ex-high school maths teacher at my boarding school and now principal of Champion Valley School. She'd come a long way. And so had I, as I had to remind myself.

'You're a part of her team now,' Dodo had said, as he counselled me before I started the job.

'Correct.'

'You shouldn't be scared of her.'

'Why would you assume I am scared of her?'

'Because she's Mrs Mehta.'

'It sounds like *you're* scared of her.'

'I'm scared *for* you.'

'How is this helping? Are you *asking* me to be scared of her?'

'I'm just saying—be yourself.'

'You're still not helping.'

'Don't be afraid.'

'I never am.'

'But be a little afraid.'

'Because she's Mrs Mehta?'

'Right, because she's Mrs Mehta. Everyone should be a little scared of her. But don't enter this relationship with any baggage.'

'She's my employer, not my lover.'
'You know what I mean.'
'I never do. And I don't know why the fuck I take any advice from you at all!'

To be fair, if it wasn't for his advice, I wouldn't have had this job. I didn't know whether to blame him or thank him, though the current theme seems to be gratitude, so I had thanked him with as little sarcasm as possible.

Presently, Mrs Mehta was signing a pile of papers, her glasses perched at the edge of her long regal nose, her starched saree clipped to her effervescent white blouse, her long hair intentionally left grey, falling neatly around her angular face. She looked like she was working very hard to save the world! So, I cleared my throat to remind her that she had the pleasure of my company and she'd have to put her superhero cape aside for just a bit.

'Sorry about this. Would you like a cup of tea?' she asked tersely, like she knew the answer would be in negative, so, I shook my head and thanked her. Evidently the etiquette training had helped. 'I'll only take a minute more, *Am*bika.'

She said '*Am*-bika', not '*Um*-bika', as my name should be pronounced.

It struck me then that there are only two reasons I can never be made a school principal. One, I don't have that crisp diction that most principals seem to possess—the one where they bite their v's and hiss their s's and cluck their t's and give everything, including names, their very own pronunciation twist, almost making you wish that you were called *Am*bika and not *Um*bika. And two, I don't have the stern-looking aquiline nose that principals seem to possess. Mine was more button-like and did not suffice for one that commanded respect.

Mrs Mehta picked up the stack of papers and tapped it against her table to align the edges before keeping it aside. Then, she interlocked her long, artistic fingers, with a glinting rock adorning one. I wondered how many of my travel plans just that one rock could finance.

'So, my dear, welcome to Champion Valley School!' her voice boomed, and I immediately sat up straighter.

'Er, I'm thankful for the opportunity,' I said carefully.

'I'm sure you will be a great asset.'

I nodded, forcing myself to smile, an expression I barely dared to use with principals in my earlier interactions.

'I just wanted you to know how much is at stake here.'

Right. Futures to shape and all. I cleared my throat and declared valiantly, 'I will try my best to—'

'To start with, you have to make sure you are aligned with the rules and regulations of Champion Valley School.'

'Of course. I've read the manual and attended—'

'You need to be here at 7.45 a.m. everyday. No leave unless sanctioned beforehand. Sick days are restricted to five. A medical certificate is required to be submitted, if you need more.'

'Yes, I'm aware of it. I've seen the—'

'Dress code is of utmost importance. No casuals. Nothing above the knee. No fancy hairstyles. No fancy accessories.'

'I wouldn't really even bother—'

'Your role here is not to befriend the parents. Nor are you here to belittle the parents. You're here as a facilitator, a partner, an educator. You're responsible for the growth and development of all your wards, with special emphasis on their mental well-being.'

It felt like it was one of those standard motivational speeches. I began to relax a little.

'CVS has a standard to uphold, and we cannot be seen as someone frivolous, especially with respect to our staff.'

It was obvious that she wanted no contribution or reassurance from me during the course of this conversation, but I had to look attentive—of which I was doing a great job, if I could say so myself.

'Our teachers and teaching methodology speak for themselves. We are a school known for its high standards of ethics. We are a school known for imparting impactful, applicable learning.'

Yes, yes and yes, it was all on the website, thank you very much. And Shilpa Anand, the Grade III coordinator, had been drilling it into our heads all of last week.

But then suddenly, Mrs Mehta leaned forward and narrowed her eyes.

'Which basically means, *Am*bika, as you would be well aware, nobody should know the *real* reason you're here.'

Lesson One
Life Sciences

From: Grade Coordinator Shilpa Anand <Shilpa.anand@cvs.in>
To: Grade III Parents Group
Date: 15 Mar 2022 at 9:31 AM
Sub: Welcome to Grade III

Dear Parents,

'Integrity is doing the right thing even when no one's watching' – C.S. Lewis

A very warm welcome to Grade III!

We have had the most delightful year watching our children acquire new academic and social skills in the year gone by, and look forward to further application of these skills in the year to come.

The class is undergoing a shuffle. Your assigned class teacher will be in touch with you shortly. We look forward to having a full house on Orientation Day, to set expectations and prepare ourselves for the fresh academic year. Please block 22 March 2022, 9 a.m., in your calendars so that we may kickstart this journey together as a team.

Just a quick update on the fabulous achievements of our CVS Junior School students this quarter:

- Karthik K. (Grade V) has won gold at the Delhi swimming meet hosted by AISA
- Reyaan Kumar and Avaan Prabhakar (Grade V) won gold at the All India Table Tennis Doubles Championship 2022
- Rhea Sharma (Grade IV), Kiera Chandok (Grade III) and Virat Sethi (Grade III) won silver at the International Art Competition 2021–22

- Syra Chhabra (Grade III) attained gold in the International SMART Learning Meet in Maths, Science and English Literature

Please join me in congratulating our young achievers.

We wish you a very restful spring break and look forward to seeing you on 22 March.

Regards,
Shilpa Anand
Coordinator, Grades III, IV & V

Riddhi

Weight: 72.5 kgs
Diet plan: Salt-free

Why do they even call it a 'diet'? Diet means food. But 'dieting' means you have no food! You just eat air. And stare and stare at photos and reels of food on Instagram. And dream about your cheat day. And count how many hours it's been since you last ate something and how many hours before you are allowed to have the low-fat, non-tasty, fistful portion of a meal.

I was so happy when I was doing keto—chicken legs with cheese and banana cake and gobhi ka pizza base and what not! But I gained three kilos. I told Harsh that 'Harsh, maybe one has to gain weight before losing', but he didn't listen. Not even when I admitted that well, in true sense, I wasn't doing full carb-free. I mean, if you don't add maida to banana cake, how it will rise? And how to eat dry chicken legs without garlic bread? And so what if you use regular Britannia white maida pizza base instead of gobhi as long as you are putting gobhi on *top* of it? It should still be okay, no?

But Harsh is too conscious. He's put me on some other diet. Some Indian guru's 'go back to roots' diet. He doesn't realize my roots are in *Punjab*! I used to have ghee poori for breakfast and malai lassi for brunch. Then aalu kulcha for second breakfast and gur halwa for second brunch. There's more butter than blood in my body and, even if I eat vegetables, they will enter my bloodstream and get deep-fried into pakodas automatically. What a nonsense diet!

But today the dietician gave me a 'salt-free' diet. Why did Gandhiji do the Dandi March for then? We could have gotten Independence from those Britishers a few years earlier only if we didn't care for salt as society! It is anti-nationalist to go salt-free! I told Harsh that, but ever since he's become broker in Gurgaon—he was in Rajouri before this, and sorry, 'real estate agent' he likes to call himself now—he thinks we must be like all Gurgaon people. Have you seen movie *Hindi Medium*? We are like that only. He is, not me. He's branded top to toe. I still buy all my clothes from Dolly Boutiques in Pitampura but he shops at Emporio: Tom Afford, Gucchi, Armani, Burglary, Versace, Tommy Hilfinger and what not. He says I should also upgrade! Well, Dolly Aunty has three-storey boutique now, instead of two, thanks to me; so how's that for upgrade!

He gets angry too much, my Harsh. If one kilo also goes up and he acts like I've become a cow. He is forgetting I'm Riddhi Makheeja Chhabra! I'll be gorgeous even if I'm 100 kilos. Abhi toh I'm only 69. Weighing machine is showing 72.5, but that's because I'm wearing a very heavy dress today. My in-laws' side is visiting, na!

I look up from the reel I was watching on Instagram on how to make healthy butter chicken—put dahi instead of butter, which means it's not butter chicken, na?—just as Syra walks in and, as it is around her, I sit up a bit straighter.

You'll all think this is very strange. Mother getting conscious in front of her seven-year-old daughter. But Syra Chhabra has that effect on everyone. By god, she's such an old soul. She just likes to read and makes all sorts of electronics. And Harsh is so impressed with her, he's made her join advanced robotics course. Plus, she's all junior Olympiad champion, and excels in all academics and all teachers are only saying 'wah-wah' to her. Even today, some email came from school with her name for some competition she won. Now all people on WhatsApp group saying 'Congy' or 'Congo' and I'm like it's okay, yaar, she's not gone to the moon or anything. Right now she's still designing the rocket, I think so.

As per me, children should be a little naughty. Not so-serious-types always. How different she is from my Shivam, who runs with NERF guns all day long and has made two drivers quit because he threw something at them—not very large or dangerous also, but from our penthouse all the way down, hawa ka force aa jaata hai. But Syra is a role-model child. Always getting medals.

'Mama, you don't have to diet, you know,' Syra says wisely, looking at my phone where the fake butter chicken reel is still playing. I immediately grab it and try to pause the video. But all fake phones have the same problem. Screen freezes. 'You just need to add healthier things to your diet. You should be comfortable with your body.'

The other thing that's scary about Syra is that all her thoughts about life are like what the people of the internet are saying, and she's not even on social media! You tell me, how can seven-year-old be feminine? I mean, feminist? She tells me just because I'm a stay-at-home mom, I should not feel secondary to Harsh in any way. It's a choice I've made. She says we should find our self-worth from within ourselves and not how people see us. She sounds like Astha TV.

'Do you want a snack, Gudiya?' I ask, hoping to change the topic.

'Nah. I just made some granola.'

See? Not a normal snack. Not 'I ate a biscuit, chocolate, cupcake'. Seven-year-old made *granola*. Wore oven mitts, and put almonds and all in the oven. I'm just surprised she didn't make the oven itself. Maybe by the time she's nine.

'Would you like some?' she asks me.

'I'll just eat a biscuit,' I say absent-mindedly, realizing later that I can't since I'm on salt-free diet, and my next meal is after thirty-seven minutes and it's cucumber which is 96 per cent water. *Beda gark!*

'Mama, I was wondering whether you could order a new pencil box? Nanima gave me ₹500 last week so ...'

I immediately pick up the phone and go to Amazon app.

'Which one you want, Gudiya?'

'Anything will do. Lalita Didi's son is starting school next week, so I wanted to gift it to her.'

I stop scrolling. Lalita Didi is the nanny who looks after my Shivam. She's very lousy because she takes too much leaves and doesn't clean his room properly, but her mother works for my mother so it's best to keep someone known only, na. Syra is very nice to her. Syra is nice to all staff.

'I gave her new pencil box last year only,' I point out.

'Yes, but we're all starting the new academic year and you only said we should have new things.'

'But that's for you!'
'Why not for him?'
'Because ...' *Hai!* I feel stomped. Sorry, stumped. I just give her the phone. 'You only see which design.'

I am irritated, but, truth is, also feet a little bit proud. Only Syra would do such things. She always cares for everyone. So kind-hearted.

If she won't run the world one day, who will?

Not that Giselle's brat, for sure.

Giselle

Time: 2.49 p.m.
Unread emails (2,478)

FFS! Was there nothing Rajiv could manage without me? I called him but, of course, he pretended like he's busier than the chief justice of India! We've had so many arguments about running one's own company is far more taxing than being a corporate lawyer, but he always left me to deal with the day-to-day shit! And shit reminded me ... Who was that fellow asking for shit loads of money? Karan? Arjun? Karan Johar? Karan Johri? Amit Johri? Samit Johri!

Mind maps. That's why they were so important. You should be able to make neuron connections to remember things. I looked for his email ID and started typing out an email, cradling my phone under my chin—as I made the third attempt to call the supreme master of my universe, but there was no response. Bloody hell, I could be hit by a bus and be dying, and he'd still be in some stupid client meeting.

> Dear Samit,
> I have an opportunity for you. It's with Bathware Pvt Ltd., who deal with sanitaryware and fittings. They are, in

your words, offering 'shit loads of money'. I thought this would fit your criteria in more ways than one!

Delete. I needed to sound more serious. Why wasn't Rajiv answering?

Dear Samit,
I have an opportunity for you with Bathware Pvt Ltd. They deal with sanitaryware and fittings. The website has been linked below. Based on our last discussion, this role may help you reach your salary ambitions.

Again, Rajiv didn't answer! I dialled a fourth time.

The role requires immersing yourself in the sanitation habits of urban and rural India to help build insights for the category.

'Get ready to immerse yourself in some serious shit!' I said out loud, holding back from typing out that one too.
'What shit?'
Shit! 'Rajiv?'
'That's who you called ...'
'Of course, I know who I called!' I snapped.
'Well, why have you called?' he asked, daring to sound exasperated.
But, fuck, now I'd forgotten why. Bloody Rajiv Savarkar—taking forever to answer and now I'd forgotten. My mind was with Samit Johri and Bathware. I desperately started looking around my desk for a clue. I always had a hundred Post-its for reminders but I had no idea which one I was looking for right now.

'Why weren't you answering your phone?' I asked crossly, buying myself time.

'I'm with a client, Gis.'

'Yes, but you know I call you only when it's important.'

'Well, what is so important then?'

God knows what it was. Client? Lead? Candidate? Maid? Our son? Our *son*! Ha! Mind maps!

'Have you paid Kevin's fee?' I said, almost barking.

'Kevin's fee?'

'Yes! The reason they allow him into Champion Valley School every morning!'

'What fee are we paying now?'

'The annual fee. I've just got a reminder that they'll be charging a 5 per cent penalty for late-fee tomorrow onwards. Last time we paid ₹18,000.'

'No, we didn't.'

'No, we didn't because I went and fought with them.'

'Why can't *you* pay it?'

'Because I'm just closing a position.' Not true. I was just starting out with it, but he didn't need to know that.

'Gis, I have a very busy day …'

'You really want to start with me on that, your honour? *Really?* Should I really enumerate the thousands of tasks I've undertaken since 5 in the morning when you were, as I recall, getting ready to play golf, a leisure sport.'

'Fine, I'll do it! On the school portal?'

'Of course, on the school portal, Rajiv! How else? Do you expect some fairy godmother to make an appearance on a magic carpet and collect a cheque from you?'

'Never a straight answer from you, Gis. I'm logging in, okay? Bye.'

I disconnected the call and cursed him, but also thanked him secretly. Then I went back to Samit Johri.

> Not only will this help you attain that leap in salary, but it will also help your future prospects by ...

My phone was ringing, and I answered Rajiv's call immediately.

'Giselle?'
'What?'
'What's our login?'
'Don't you know the login?'
'Would I be asking if I knew?'
'Well, I don't know it either!'
'Don't you access the portal regularly?'
'Do *you* access the portal regularly?'
'No.'
'So any reason you think I would?'
'Forget it. I've found an admin email on the website. I'm mailing them.'

He disconnected before I could, always a sore point with me if the other person disconnects first, and I gnashed my teeth. As if he was doing me a favour by paying the fee for *our* son! I turned back to my email.

> ... having experience in rural India makes you a worthy candidate with a lot of FMCG companies including the ones you'd mentioned ...

'Gis, what section is Kevin in?'
'What section of what?'
'Kevin! I need to know his class and section for the email.'
'Just say Grade II, Rajiv! They'll track him down.'
'Okay, but do you not know which section he's in?'
'Of course I do!'

'Then what is it?'
'Find it out yourself!'
I disconnected first this time and felt a whole lot better.

... during our interaction. We strongly believe that this experience will make you ...

'Gis, I figured it out and thought you should know too. He's in B.'
'Of course I knew that!'
'You didn't.'
'I did! I knew he's in II B.'
'He's in III B. He was in II A. See, you didn't know.'
'Neither did you!'
'Yes, but—'
'But I should know because I'm the mother? Isn't that what you were about to say?'
'No, but you always claim you're so on top of things.'
'I *am* on top of things! I'm the one who knew the fee is overdue.'
'Fair enough. You win.'
'Of course I do.'
'We should swap professions. I should be a head-hunter and you'll certainly make a great lawyer.'
'For someone who took four tries to get through on the phone, you sure have a lot of time on hand now, Rajiv, for this chit-chat.'
'I do now. I'm done with my meeting and heading home. Where's Kev?'
'Where do you think he'll be?'

Pareeta

Week 4

'How is it?'
I knew there was no point asking him because he was the sweetest boy in the world and he'd only sing praises, but he loved to be on my tasting committee and, really, there was no better judge for a chocolate-covered breakfast cereal than this round-faced, cherry-cheeked boy with his button nose and Harry Potter glasses.

'Hmmmmm! It's amazing, Aunty!' Kevin Savarkar, my son's best friend, replied, while little bits of the cereal fell out of his mouth straight into his lap.

'My Mama baked it herself!' Aryan said proudly, serving himself a spoonful and I patted his head lovingly.

'Mama's always got something in the oven,' Vidya said slyly from the top of her bowl. I shot her a warning look and turned back to the children just as Aryan innocently said, 'Not always. Sometimes she cooks on the gas stove also.'

'Oh, she has a secret oven she hasn't told you about,' Vidya told him snarkily. Teenage daughters are the bane of their mother's existence. And mine was forever poised for a fight. We fought like siblings, with slamming doors and shouting matches, and there was more drama between mothers and teenage daughters than the Korean television industry could ever account for. I took a deep breath to calm myself down before smiling at the boys again, and reminded myself that this time Vidya's was a natural reaction. I was just being harsh.

'It's like you suddenly remember you can have babies every seven years!' Vidya had said when I told her I was expecting again.

A third one on the way! Not like anyone could tell because it had barely been a month, but I could tell because of the waves of nausea I felt. I hadn't even intended on doing a test but Vidya had walked in when I'd been talking to Pankaj. Such theatrics had unfolded. It was the reaction parents reserved for unmarried girls who'd fallen pregnant in our generation—but to get it from your own daughter? That was a bit too much. I truly hoped I'd have a boy this time because I could not handle another teenage girl in the house and that reaction from her had sealed it; I was certainly having this child.

'Aunty?' Kevin said with his mouth full, again spraying my tablecloth with his half-eaten chocolate cereal and germs. I ran a damp cloth on it before he continued. 'Can you please bake some muffins for me tomorrow?'

'She's not baking anything for you!' Vidya chided him. 'You don't pay her, you little imp!'

'What's an "imp"?'

'Important person,' I said quickly and glared at Vidya, who just shrugged. These boys could do without vocabulary lessons from an angsty teenager, thank you very much. 'Of course I can bake you muffins, Kevin. What's the occasion?'

'It's my birthday.'

'Your birthday's in June,' Aryan corrected him.

'It's not my birth month, but it's my birth date.'

'You're just looking for an excuse to eat more cake,' Vidya told him. 'Fatso!'

'Vidya!' I shrieked.

'I'll pay you,' Kevin offered. 'I'll ask my mother to pay you.'

'Oh? You've remembered you have a mother? It'll be nice of you to go home once in a while,' Vidya told him snarkily.

'Vidya, that's enough! Of course I'll bake for you, Kevin. I don't take money from family and you're family to us.'

'Yup. We're a family that just keeps growing and growing,' Vidya said with a sigh.

'Vidya!'

'I did ask Mom if I can tell you to bake,' Kevin continued innocently, 'because it's also her anniversary.'

'Oh, is it? Happy anniversary to them! In fact, I'll bake you a whole cake, Kevin. Why just muffins?'

'It's not my father's anniversary. Only my mother's.'

Vidya immediately sat up, interested. 'What do you mean?'

'It's her work anniversary. When she started her own company.'

Vidya looked deflated, as if that wasn't the scoop she was looking for. I smiled at Kevin.

'Oh, that's so sweet! And so nice of you to remember,' I said.

'She's been going on and on about it. She says it's such a waste of time, but will need to take her team out for lunch.'

'Well, it's very nice of her. Please tell her I will do it.'

I sat down in the corner and made note of it. I ran Pareeta's Pastries, a home-baking business that had flourished well in the last few years. I typically did all my baking in the morning the minute the children were in school and had good staff to support me with my deliveries. My heart skipped a beat as it struck me that I wouldn't have that luxury in a few months from now, with a new baby in the house. Was I really ready for this? I was forty-two, after all. A successful entrepreneur, already with so much on my hands. The situation was so different from when Aryan was conceived and I was on a career break. Pankaj was also so hands-on back then. Now, we were in a long-distance marriage. And, somewhere in my head, I knew this pregnancy was to—

'Isn't it, Mom?'

I jumped to see Aryan and Kevin both looking at me.

'Sorry? What were you saying?'

'We're asking if we'll have a new student in class now that Chirag has moved to Deadmark.'

'It's "Denmark",' Vidya corrected them.

'Copper Heaven,' Kevin specified.

'Copenhagen. I'm sure you will,' I replied as I heard the oven timer go off. 'Champion Valley always has such a long waiting list.'

Vidya sighed wisely. 'Yet another privileged brat.'

Kainaz

	Ten points on Delhi/Gurgaon:
1.	Pollution: It's the first thing you associate with the capital region, but it literally hits you as soon as you land. The smokiness in the air. The ash-like dust that stings your eyes. The itchy skin. The persistent need to cough. School brochures mentioning brand of air purifiers used in classrooms. I'd always thought the whole scenario was exaggerated. But it's not. It's 100 per cent true.
2.	Traffic: You don't measure distances in kms but in minutes. Google maps doesn't show red patches on roads, it shows blue patches. There are more potholes than roads. As long as you have a vehicle, you can drive it wherever you want—road or no road.
3.	Weather: Dry, scorching hot summer. The doom of biting cold winters. Two separate wardrobes for two separate and extreme seasons. And a whole new fashion mandate to keep up with too.
4.	Appearances: Of buildings and people, both blindingly jazzy. Not a hair out of place, not a hair on your face. There's a clear dominance of looks over substance. The need to glisten more brightly than the other, make sure you're as intimidating as possible.
5.	Sense of entitlement: The

'Mama, what are you writing?'

I snapped my notebook shut.

'Another one of your lists?'

'Nothing of the sort, Ahaan.'

'Daddy says one day we'll earn a lot of money by publishing your lists.'

Daddy. Varaz. The reason we were in Delhi. Gurgaon, to be precise.

'Daddy's such a joker. What do you want?'

'Mama, I can't find Iggy. I found Piggy and Tiggy, but not Iggy. Is it in one of your boxes?'

That my seven-year-old still played with stuffed toy animals unlike the Xbox-wielding kids of Delhi was another reason I didn't want to be here.

'I haven't seen it, but we still have some cartons to unpack.'

He perched himself on my knee and sighed. 'We've been unpacking for ten days. I'm bored. And every time I think it's one of my boxes, more of your stuff falls out.'

I tapped his chin. 'What an exaggerator! I only had two boxes.'

'And I opened both of them.'

'Well I'm glad you did because we were able to put up some nice paintings!' Never mind that I'd almost taken the wall down while trying to smack in a nail and had emerged from the room looking like Casper, covered in a cloud of cement, but the paintings were up and the walls looked better. More liveable, somehow.

'Can I call Roshan now?' he asked eyeing my phone.

'You just spoke to him an hour ago.'

'But I'm so bored.'

He looked so distressed that I pulled him into a hug. 'Why don't you go downstairs and cycle around? Maybe you'll make some new friends.'

'I don't want new friends. I want my old friends. I want Roshan!'

I knew exactly how he felt. I wanted my old friends, too. And it hadn't even been two weeks.

'Come, let's go open some more boxes. Maybe we'll find Iggy.'

Hand in hand, we walked to the living area where the boxes were stacked in a corner. He stopped suddenly to look at the Van Gogh imitation I'd hung up.

'I didn't realize it was so big,' he said innocently.

It wasn't. It just looked bigger in our smaller flat. Of course, nothing would compare to our beautiful sea-facing bungalow in Majorda, Goa, but the little pieces of art did make this 1800 sq. ft apartment a bit more cheerful. Especially since the residents of the flat were anything but cheerful currently.

We ripped the tape off one of the cartons, but it revealed only a bunch of papers. Ahaan spotted something and almost fell into the carton trying to pull it out. It was his old school ID card. My heart sank. School. Or rather the lack of it. My top reason for not liking Delhi. I needed to add that to my list.

We had been searching for a suitable school for months since we learnt of our move. Some schools had responded positively and asked us, very conveniently, to make a small donation (equivalent to the cost of a brand new bus) to gain admission, but with the others we were soldiering on—going for tests and interviews, and trying to act like model parents. We had to align on a vision for our child, on the values we wanted to instil as a family, on the importance of becoming contributing members to society. Because apparently just wanting your child out of your bed and in his own room wasn't a parenting goal enough.

I missed the comfort of our old St. Jon's school back in Goa. I had walked across when Ahaan had turned four and asked Mrs Lucy if he could join them the following month and she had said, 'Of course', because he was like family. Everyone was family there. Then she'd offered me a cup of tea and we'd chatted about all my cousins who had graduated from St. Jon's like me, and I'd left with a little gate pass to let him in the very next day. But here we were, running from pillar to post being told we were on the coveted 'waitlist' with no respite in sight.

Varaz was still hopeful we would make it somewhere, but I had little optimism left. Maybe it was for the best if we didn't get admission anywhere and I would just have to drag our sorry asses back to Goa.

As if he could hear me thinking of him, Varaz's name lit up my phone screen.

'K, good news. Ahaan's been accepted into Champion Valley School.'

I was suddenly speechless, my heart pounding, barely believing what I had just heard. Champion Valley School? We'd been told it was impossible to find a place in it. Even though the interview had gone well, I had written it off completely.

'But ... how?' I managed to ask.

'Well, I had to sleep with the owner but it was worth it.'

'Very funny, Varaz!'

He started laughing and so did I. The relief was overwhelming. I think I had tears in my eyes. Gosh, Champion Valley School! Who would have thought? It was as if a huge weight had been lifted off my shoulders. As if now everything would sort itself out after all. I looked down at Ahaan, who had miraculously chanced upon Iggy.

Jia

> Hey Mother India! I'm going to be late.

> No surprises there! It's midnight.

> I was on a call with HO. I just saw your missed call.

> I didn't call

> Rabia?

> Maybe

> Is she asleep?

> It's midnight!

> Doesn't answer my question

> 📎 Photo

> I was right. Still jumping about. Tell her I'm running late

> That's 3 nights in a row

> No shit

More people with you?

> Yes

Including that Roddy fellow?

> No

Good!

> He had to go home early

Ok. Gnite.

Don't leave the keys in the door

Double lock when you reach

> I'm 34!

Talk to me when you stop leaving the keys in the door

> So the reason Roddy left early is because I punched him

What?

What????

WHAT?????

> Answer the phone

>> No. I'm with colleagues

> What happened?

>> He asked me out. I punched him.

>> And he's such a twat, one little punch and his nose started bleeding

> Oh my god! Jia!

>> What! You also told me he sounded like a jerk!

> I said he sounded interested!

> You shouldn't have done it! You should have just gone to your human resource team!

>> No. I can't have anything on record till the divorce

>> I have to have full custody of Rabia

> I don't know what to say

>> Nothing is good. Gnite!

> Will you please drive home safe?

>> No. I'll drive like a maniac

> I'm serious. This is not New York

>> No? You could've fooled me!

> Gurgaon is unsafe. Ask someone to follow you

>> What a thing to wish for!

> Ask someone KNOWN to follow you!

>> I'm not 18!

> You look 18

>> With belly fat. Gnite Mom.

> BTW, your friend Riddhi had called to check if you've paid Rabia's fee? Today was the last day

>> So impressed you know what BTW stands for! Gnite!

Lesson Two
Social Sciences

From: Ambika S <Ambika.s@cvs.in>
To: Grade III B Parents Group
Date: 20 Mar 2022 at 9:31 AM
Sub: Welcome to III B

Dear Parents,

Welcome to III B.

PFA the Grade III orientation presentation.

Look forward to meeting you all tomorrow.

Regards,
Ambika S.
Class Teacher, III B

Ambika

So, I got into trouble. On day minus one. I realized my welcome email to the parents was about fifty words, while the other class teachers wrote lengthy essays of about five hundred words. With sentences like, 'While we teach children about life, children teach us what life is all about.'

That's right. I thought all the other teachers were poetic geniuses till I realized they'd copied their lines straight off the internet. And I hadn't even signed off with our values, 'Integrity, Perseverance and Consciousness'.

I understood my blunder when I went to school to prepare for the orientation—we were forced to do so—and Shilpa Anand, the coordinator for Grades III, IV and V, came to check on something just as I pressed 'send' on my email. I thought I saw her heart physically leap out of her mouth. It wasn't a pretty sight.

'It's fine! It's fine!' she told herself and even started patting her chest like 'All is Well'. She sat down next to me—more like collapsed on the chair next to me, but more of her melodrama later.

'I'll share some emails that have been sent by the other teachers so that you have an idea for next time,' she offered helpfully, as a bead of sweat appeared on her upper lip, which was, incidentally, in desperate need for laser treatment. I had no idea what she was talking about. We'd been asked to send an invitation and I thought my email did the job pretty decently.

'Always start your emails with something inspiring. Or cheerful. Never a joke, no. That's against our ethos. But something that makes parents feel proud to be a part of CVS.'

That's when she showed me the email that started with the inspirational quote.

'And write something more engaging. Tell them a little about yourself. Tell them about the year ahead. Compel them to come to school and be involved with their child's education. Motivate them, let them take ownership!'

'Er ... In an email?'

'Yes.' She scrolled through her phone and handed me another example of what had been sent. It looked like an essay. I would never read the whole thing if I were a parent!

'I'll make a note,' I lied politely, handing her phone back.

'Right. So, anyway, the reason I'm here is to tell you that we'll split the day into two. In the first half you prepare your individual classrooms, as discussed. I'm sure you have some great ideas.' I had no clue what she meant by that. 'And, in the second half, we'll do the halls.'

I was even more lost if it was possible. 'We'll do what in the halls?' I asked tentatively. I had visuals of me participating in a flash mob.

'Set them up. Remember we were debating themes for welcoming students back for a new academic year last week?'

'Yes ...?'

'Well, we chose the "Gardens of Wisdom" theme and we're going to execute it today.'

Before I could ask exactly how we were expected to *execute* it, she sauntered away to the next classroom.

What on earth did she mean by 'prepare your classroom'?

I looked around at the furniture and very meaningfully said, 'Be ready, you guys! Tough year ahead.'

I looked around and had a flashback of my own school days. How many tables were ruined with compass scratches? How many tiffins were eaten hidden under the desks? How many seats were changed every time someone got caught talking? And what exactly did we use those bulletin boards for? The timetable? A list of students in the classroom? I decided to walk to the other classrooms and get some inspiration.

Sahiba Kulkarni, Miss, had just been promoted from being a Kindergarten teacher to Grade III and was standing on a step ladder hanging up some streamers. Was there a birthday party I was unaware of?

'Oh, hello, Miss Ambika. Looking for something?'

In my short interaction with Sahiba over the last few weeks, I was surprised to learn that some people smiled this much, even without any dopamine-inducing substance in their bloodstream. She looked like she could bounce on air and blow petals off her palm, and generally whip up candyfloss with a wave of her hand. And keeping up with that aspect of her personality, her classroom looked like it had fallen out of an illustrated fairytale book. The origami birds looked so real that I was surprised they hadn't flown at my face yet.

'Um ... I was wondering,' I asked, 'whether you knew what Shilpa wants us to do in the classrooms?'

She paused but didn't let that Barbie-doll smile fall off her face. 'What do you mean? We need to do up the classrooms.'

'But what does *that* mean?'

'You need to beautify them, set them up, organize, arrange ... Anything to welcome the students for the coming term.'

'Right.' God! Just like I'd dreaded. More work. I thanked her and marched back to my own classroom.

I'd always thought teachers did lesser work than in other professions, but I had spent literally every day from eight in the morning till four in the evening working—trainings, assignments, planning, executing. All while people like Dodo, who had a high-flying consultant job and was living it up in Australia, acted like he hated it and couldn't wait to get back at the end of the six-month contract. But then he would post pictures on Instagram every day, looking quite the opposite of hating it. Yes, I had an Instagram account which was locked and that I used only for snooping. I am not a social media person. But, even if I were, what would I post now? Images of blackboards? Homework sheets? Multiplication hacks? And, come to think of it, I was considered brighter than him at one point in time.

'Should've thought of that before you dropped out of college,' Dodo's words rang in my ears.

It was my postgrad, to be fair. All cool people dropped out of postgrad. I was waiting to become Zuckerberg and Gates and Steve Jobs and ... Oh god. Those guys were all in tech and I sucked at it. Perhaps that's where I went wrong. I should have studied coding rather than the six languages I had learnt in junior school.

Anyway, I had a room to decorate and all that. And that too without an interior decorator. How did one even do that? I decided to start by researching 'classroom decorations' on the internet. Sure, there were plenty of suggestions for kindergarten classrooms, but Grade III? What were eight-year-olds like anyway?

After three hours of searching—okay, I may have gone astray a few times—I made a blueprint of sorts. I'd have one wall for academics, one wall for achievements and I'd paste 'Integrity, Perseverance, Consciousness' in the middle of it all in a gigantic font that would take care of the entire third wall. I just had to get the font size right. I had to admit, I spent an inordinate amount of time finalizing the font type and settled on Calibri after all, but at least it looked serious and imposing.

I then divided the academic wall into four quadrants and wrote a subject name each. Then I printed a nice image for science and maths, and pinned that up too. The achievements wall was, of course, blank since there were no achievements here but again Google images came to the rescue. I found a picture of a boy holding up a medal while another one looked at him angrily. Perhaps not the most useful image to have since it bordered on jealousy, but I couldn't be bothered to look for any more. Since I was also all out of creativity by now, I printed out the timetable and class list, and pinned those up as well. My classroom looked pretty damn full and I felt a huge wave of pride.

With a definite sense of satisfaction, I sat down to check my email. There were about twenty from Shilpa Anand, who, in my opinion, really needed to get a life—such a micromanager—and the rest from travel websites that I had subscribed to and didn't want spamming my personal ID.

I was just learning the benefits of owning a women's travel card from one of the banks, when I heard a gasp and there she was standing at the doorway.

'You haven't even started!' Shilpa Anand cried.

I looked around me. 'What do you mean?'

'Your walls are bare!'

Was she blind? I decided to defend myself. 'No, they aren't. I've organized them.'

'But there's nothing here according to the lesson plan. We discussed the lesson plan all week. You could have done something in line with that! Put up the vocabulary list we have this term, write something on the values and ... No, no, no, Miss Ambika. No Google images! We at CVS pride ourselves in everything handmade. Please draw these pictures.'

Draw? Fuck no. She had to be kidding.

'But do you like the quadrants?' I pushed my luck.

She looked at me as if I were crazy, but then turned away, looking very perturbed. She started chewing on her lower lip. 'Uh, it's very ... orderly,' she said at last.

My smile was bathed in sarcasm. 'Thank you.'

'It's very symmetrical. Very organized,' she continued. 'Like, very neat. So ... methodical.'

Clearly, everyone at CVS seemed to be thesaurus-friendly.

'But these are eight-year-olds!' she blurted. 'This is too black and white! Did you see Sahiba's room? Why don't you take her help in cheering this up a little?'

'But her room looked like kindergarten.'

'Exactly! Why not transport children back to their happiest days!'

'Why, are they not happy now?'

'No, what I mean is …'

See? She didn't have an answer. Then she changed the subject and continued to look pretty pained. 'Miss Ambika, have you been through the orientation deck? You haven't sent in any queries.'

Orientation deck? The one we sent to the parents? Why was I supposed to read it?

'Um …'

She visibly panicked. She took a deep breath—something she seemed to do a lot around me—and then marched purposefully to my desk. Without my permission, she scrolled through my email and opened the relevant document.

'Here, please have a read. This is imperative.'

'Yes, I was meaning to,' I lied.

'You must know every word on the presentation. They'll ask you questions. Anticipate them. Note them down. Ask me. We all need to be unified in the response we offer.'

Why did it sound like a battle, this orientation with parents?

As if reading my mind, she said, 'You cannot face those parents without fully preparing yourself. You have no idea of the sort of things that happen.'

God, she was a worrier. I shrugged. 'I'm sure it won't be that bad.'

'No, Miss Ambika,' she said looking at me seriously in the eye. 'It will be worse.'

Kainaz

	Three reasons Champion Valley School intimidated me:
1.	The building: It looked like Buckingham Palace. When I'd first seen the dome and columns and the giant emblem shining atop, I'd had this ridiculous urge to curtsy. It was simply iridescent! The woodwork was expensive, well-polished, well-maintained and the ambient lights made everything look so much glossier. You could place a throne and a red carpet, and it wouldn't look out of place. Such a huge contrast from St. Jon's School in Goa, which looked like it hadn't seen a coat of paint since pre-Independence days and one would have to walk around wondering which of the creaking fans would fall on one next.
2.	The people: The average parent in CVS was so well turned out, you could be walking down the sets of *Emily in Paris*. Women in crisp designer clothes, wearing fancy sunglasses, carrying bags that shouted brand names. Men in sharp suits and shiny pointy shoes, who spoke into their snazzy cell phones cracking, no doubt, million-dollar deals. Even in my brand-new Lycra slacks paired with my favourite pink kurta that I had painfully accessorized with a chunky silver necklace, I felt totally like the odd one out.

3.	The teachers: Most un-teacherlike. They were young and fit, and wore the smartest business casuals. Even the odd one in ethnic wear looked straight out of a magazine. So unlike our matrons back at St. Jon's, who wore their sarees on their chest and looked like they were born to teach. Even though they all smiled genially at me here, I was so nervous of having to talk to them.

As I walked down the corridor in a sea of unfamiliar faces, I felt a pang of loneliness. In a crowd this size, no matter where I was in Goa, I would have spotted a neighbour, an aunt, a cousin, a friend, an acquaintance, a classmate, my grocer, my dentist, but, here, I knew no one. My heart banged in my chest as I realized Ahaan would know no one either. I had a sudden urge to whip him up into my arms protectively and leave. It was another thing that he was with a friend of ours currently and was yet to see the school he'd be joining.

An orientation! I'd only seen those in colleges. And here, they did one annually and would take us through what we could expect for our children. Very kind of them. They never bothered with that sort of thing in St. Jon's.

I walked around like a lost soul till I finally located Ahaan's new class and stood outside the glossy doors.

'May I come in?' I knocked.

Suddenly, all the chatter in the classroom died and a lady in a printed, sleeveless kurta on jeans flipped around to look at me. She had an asymmetrical short haircut, a tall, lean body, prominent cheekbones and beautiful dark eyes. She looked nothing like a class teacher. Yet, here she was, Miss Ambika S., as her email had said.

'Of course! Please, come in. No need to knock,' she said directing me to the chairs in the classroom.

Many faces turned to look at me curiously at first and then dismissively, going back to their private conversations. I blushed as I realized that the permission at the door was totally unnecessary. I was a parent, not a student, after all! I plastered on a weak smile and walked towards the empty seats in the middle of the room. As I started inching towards a vacant one in the third row, a woman with very bleached hair and a shimmery purple blouse flashed a bright lipsticked smile at me. 'Sorry, I reserve it for my friend.'

Embarrassed, I walked to the row behind her and was about to take a seat next to a gentleman when a very agitated-looking lady in a business suit nudged past me and planted herself there, talking on her phone. She looked up at me with her cat-green eyes and, momentarily, I thought she would apologise. But she just blinked, as if wondering what I was still doing there, and went back to her telephonic conversation. I timidly walked to the row behind her, my cheeks aflame.

The teacher rapped on her table for attention. 'Good morning, everyone.'

The conversation died down and everyone sat up straight, all except the rude woman with cat eyes who had bulldozed past me and now continued to speak noisily on the phone. The gentleman next to her, possibly her husband, elbowed her, so she had the grace to lower her voice, but she kept speaking nonetheless. The class teacher knitted her eyebrows and we all watched on till she caught the lady's eye who looked slightly exasperated at being stared at but finally concluded, 'Sure. Sure. Okay I have to go now. But email me the details on giselle.savarkar@hirearchy.com. That's H-I-R-E … Never mind. I'll text you. Bye!'

I was amazed at her audacity—but I guess that was all of Delhi, wasn't it? Pushing their luck as far as they could. Pretending to be busier than they really were.

Some of the other parents openly glared at the cat-eyed lady for keeping them waiting but she looked unperturbed as she started to send a text, eyes still not on the teacher. If it had been the nuns of the yesteryears who had taught people like me, she would have had a chalk flung on her by now. Miss Ambika, however, only raised an eyebrow slightly before turning amicably to the rest of the class.

'Good morning, everyone. Thank you for coming in. My name is Ambika, er, Miss Ambika, and I'll be teaching Grade III-B.' She looked down at a piece of paper she was holding and I realized it was a cue card. 'A fresh new year is always very exciting as we chart out together a whole new development year for our children. I'll quickly take you through our presentation.'

Immediately a hand shot up. 'How long will it take? I have a meeting at ten.'

Miss Ambika stared at him as if debating whether to be polite or snap. 'Why don't we start and we'll see how it goes?' she said curtly.

'But still. Approximately?'

'Half an hour.'

'Okay.'

Not a 'thank you'. Just 'okay'. Oh, these Delhi people.

'So, welcome to III B,' she said moving to the opening slide just as another hand shot up.

'On what basis has shuffling been done?' someone whose sindoor ran down till the bridge of her nose asked.

'Why don't we first go through the PowerPoint and then I can take questions at the end?' the teacher suggested. There were some murmurs of disapproval from the parents, but she held her head high and continued to talk.

'So, very quickly, CVS was founded in 1994. Our founder, the late Mr Krishna Saraogi, along with his son, Anil Saraogi, had a vision of providing quality, experiential education to the youth and started with a small campus of 110 students in Gurgaon, er, Gurugram, which has now grown to 2,000 students. This year is special as we will be celebrating our twenty-eighth anniversary. The theme of the year is "Change" and a lot of our focus will be in getting our students to be comfortable with change.'

'Is that why the school timings are changing?' someone asked.

'What?' Miss Ambika asked, as surprised as I felt with that question.

'The school timing,' the parent continued. 'It was earlier from 8 a.m., but the new timetable says 7.50 a.m. ...'

'Right.' She looked like she was consulting a list of FAQs before she answered. 'Yes, it's being shifted by ten minutes due to traffic rule changes in our area as was communicated a few months ago.'

'But ten minutes is also too much!' someone complained.

'We won't be able to finish breakfast,' someone else complained.

'I'm not the right person to be raising this with. You can write directly to our principal, Mrs Mehta, or to the administration head for any such issues. Moving on—'

'Will lunch timings be changed? Because the children get very hungry,' someone else asked.

'And what about the lunch menu? We'd requested for less dessert in school lunches.'

'I'd actually personally asked whether we can include feta and watermelon salad during the summer months as it has great cooling properties. I'm a nutritionist and—'

'Why don't we do this?' Miss Ambika interrupted assertively. 'Why don't we take questions at the end of the session?' She was certainly a bit short on patience, though, to be fair, they were all cascading into just about everything. 'Continuing with the theme of change, the other change will be in terms of the curriculum for maths. This year we will …'

I didn't understand a word of it. Apparently, they were following one methodology, now they were following something else. Again, the parents didn't want to hold on to questions till the end. They had multiple points of view on it while I struggled to make sense of it at all and the only one who looked as stumped as me was Miss Ambika.

That's when there was a knock on the door.

'I'm so sorry I'm late. May I come in?'

Every single set of eyes turned towards the door; some mouths fell agape and there were a few audible gasps. Even the teacher changed colour as she stared at him. In complete silence, as their eyes followed him, he walked to the back of the classroom, the cat-eyed lady shifting as if to make place next to her. But he walked to the row behind and took a seat beside me.

I wasn't surprised, really. My husband, Varaz Dotwalla, had that effect on people.

Riddhi

Weight: 73 kgs
Diet Plan: Salad and soup. With exception of cookies at school orientation.
Planned: 2
Consumed: 6

But who cares about weight and all! When you realize new parent in class is none other than Varaz Dotwalla! I toh sent a message on the family WhatsApp immediately! Popularly known as Mihir Gondal from *We Are the Gondals* serial on Star Plus from about fifteen years ago, Varaz Dotwalla had been, hai, everyone's heartthrob. When he had died in serial, I thought I had also died. I cried, Mummy cried, even my maid Sarita took a week off to moan. Mourn. Whatever. And here he was. In flesh and blood! Alive! And still with his famous dimple. And muscle. Lot of muscle. Sitting five inches away from me. I toh made it sound on family WhatsApp group like he was in my lap only!

'Dekha, how Giselle shifted to make place for him?' I cackled to Jia sitting next to me, but she just rolled her eyes. Jia clearly didn't know who Varaz Dotwalla was. She must have been in US when *We Are the Gondals* was coming on TV.

'Control, yaar, Riddhi!' Harsh whispered pushing sharp elbow into my ribs. I snapped right back at him.

'Control weight, control diet, now control eyes also! You be useful now, Harsh, just pretend you're taking a pic of me and take his photo in background.'

'Are you mad! How can I take your picture during the orientation?'

'See? That Rekha Tandon toh is shamelessly taking his photo thinking nobody's seeing.' There she was, her sindoor so much, it always looked like she had head injury, putting her phone under the table but taking photo candidly. I knew these tricks! Once I'd done it with Hema Malini when she was in Dubai.

Teacher was going on and on, and nobody was even asking questions now. Whole class attention was on Varaz Dotwalla. Out of pity feeling, I turned back to teacher. Even she looked distracted. Who wouldn't be? Vaise, she looked too young to be teacher. But all teachers of Champion Valley looked younger than their age. Even Miss Veena, last year's class teacher for Syra, I thought so she was too young but her elder one was in Yell University. Miss Ambika looked younger than that also. I looked for a wedding ring on her finger but didn't find one. But nowadays modern women don't wear rings also. How is one to tell!

I looked around the room at other wedding rings, especially Varaz Dotwalla's wife's. Uff, if only I'd let her sit next to me instead of saving place for Jia! But her ring was a plain band with diamonds. Not even solitaire. Maybe it was new trend. My eyes fell on Giselle Savarkar, sitting behind me wearing olive-green business suit and heels so high like Qutab Minar, hair like brown-brown hay and skin so white-white with American-type freckle also. And her eyes also were green, like a cat everyone said, but I think so more like leopard, ready to attack. She was also in only simple gold band. Trying to be too much modern.

'Where are you lost! Pay attention!' Harsh whispered harshly. So boring this talk about homework. Syra finished it in school only. Too tough being mother of genius.

Then, it started. Same introduction game they play every year. I'm total bore of it. Miss Ambika held a stuffed ball and started to throw it towards parents. Introduce yourself and your child by comparing them to an animal. Hain? Animal? Bhai, is this school or zoo?

First went to Rekha Tandon sindoorwali. She looked so surprised and irritated to have to turn back from leching at Varaz Dotwalla, she quickly said her son was like lion because he was brave, which was rubbish. Last year at Syra's birthday party he got scared of the clown and cried.

Next, Anita Chatterjee said her daughter is nightingale. I have heard her daughter sing. More like a crow, but you can't tell a parent that. Parents are too much sensitive about children. Then Pooja Sood said their daughter was like a butterfly and I thought so she still looked like a caterpillar only, behen. No blooming had happened yet. But Pooja Sood was Harsh's client and had bought very big villa two months ago, so I couldn't say anything. Because with big villa came big pool and it was good for playdates. You can wear beachwear without being on beach.

Ball went to two more people before coming to snooty Giselle Savarkar, who almost dropped her phone. She passed it to her husband, Rajiv Savarkar who's some hi-fi lawyer, I remember, and he said his son, Kevin, was a horse, but then immediately Giselle Savarkar snatched the ball and said, 'No, he's not, he's a unicorn.' She almost shouted! He's unique and she wants him to defy stereotypes.

Bhai, you defy stereotypes first then! You kept your husband's last name very nicely, Giselle Savarkar. That is stereotype. I still say I'm Riddhi *Makheeja* Chhabra—RMC. Harsh says I sound like American rapper but why keep only your husband's name? And she wants son to defy stereotype!

Really, she is so sada hua like she eats raw lemons for breakfast. Harsh says lemons in the morning are good for weight loss but I told him lemons are only good on top of chaat or in cake. But this Giselle Savarkar …

She caught me looking at her and, with a bored expression, threw the ball right in my face!

Bloody bitch!

Pareeta

Week 4

Everyone seemed to have found their tongue only once Varaz Dotwalla left the classroom after the orientation. I walked up to introduce myself personally to the new class teacher and give her my card, in case she ever wanted to order anything for the class, but I was soon pushed aside by all these aggressive parents who wanted to know why their bus route had changed and what the school's plan was on the competitive exams policy this year and had a thousand questions on the new tab policy. The teacher looked so hassled, I walked away quietly, only to be accosted by a fuming Riddhi.

'Why you are friends with this Giselle Savarkar? She's such a rude lady!'

'What happened?'

'Didn't you see how she threw the ball to me? No decency to say sorry also!'

I calmed her down and told her she was very nice once you got to know her to which Riddhi swore she would never like to. Then I suggested we do a quick coffee meet with the new set of mommies since the class had just got shuffled and it would be nice to get acquainted with them. I always liked to mingle as it helped develop my business and I knew Riddhi liked socializing because it helped develop her social life.

She grunted that she already knew everyone and, to be fair, she looked like she did, but, on second thoughts, she was always looking for an excuse to cheat on her diet. And also to get to know Varaz Dotwalla's wife. We turned to her and she looked totally oblivious to the fairy dust her husband had sprinkled over all the women in class.

'Hello, I'm Pareeta!' I introduced myself.

She looked up as if surprised that someone had noticed her. 'Hi, I'm Kainaz.'

Large round eyes, unkempt frizzy hair, a small, petite mouth, mismatched outfit. I thought celebrity wives were supposed to be more glamorous.

'Your husband is Varaz Dotwalla?' Riddhi asked from behind me. Trust Riddhi to be so direct.

'Yes,' Kainaz said, almost embarrassed. 'You know him?'

'Hai, *everyone* knows him! Mihir from *We Are the Gondals*. You are also acting?'

'I'm not acting.'

'No, she means are you an actor?' I clarified.

'No, I'm not.'

We waited, but she didn't tell us what she did, which meant Riddhi leapt to a conclusion.

'It's okay. I am also a housewife.'

'Oh, uh, I'm not exactly a ...'

'Even Pareetaji is. She's housewife but she's also baker. She has Pareeta's Pastries on Instagram. You should try my favourite, blueberry cake. Are you on school WhatsApp group?'

Kainaz looked dazed. 'Uh ... no.'

'We'll just add you,' I said politely. 'We were just heading out for coffee. Would you like to join us?'

She agreed.

'Myself Riddhi Makheeja Chhabra,' Riddhi said pushing me aside to befriend the celebrity wife. 'Your name Kainaz? Very nice name. Shah Rukh Khan sir said in *Om Shanti Om*, "Itni shiddat se maango ke kainaz bhi sab kuch de de!"'

'That's "kainaat",' I corrected. 'She is Kainaz.'

'Achha, achha. So you are moving from Bombay? Varazji doing movie here? Serial? Reality show? Oh! Is he on *Bigg Boss*? I'll vote for him.'

'No, actually we have moved from Goa. And Varaz doesn't act any more. He's with a corporate.'

'Oho, oho!' Riddhi tutted loudly and I wanted to hide in shame. 'So sad, so sad. Where in Goa did you stay? I've been many times.'

'Majorda.'

'Which resort is that?'

'Um ... It's not a resort. It's a locality.'

'Achha, we only stay at Taj.'

I had to literally steer Riddhi out by her elbow.

'So what do you do, Kainaz?' I asked politely.

'I'm a carpenter.'

I almost dropped my phone and Riddhi stopped walking.

'I don't know what it means in Goanese,' Riddhi said, 'but here carpenter means mistri. They make furnitures.'

'I do.' Just then the other mums enveloped her and started making small talk as we walked to the café. Riddhi and I exchanged glances, and she pulled me to walk at a distance from the group.

'Hai!' Riddhi tutted next to me in a hushed voice. 'Varaz Dotwalla married a carpenter? He must be having very bad time. I have heard how celebrities become so poor nowadays.'

But we didn't realize how poor till we finished our coffees and waited for our cars. That's when Kainaz Dotwalla said goodbye, and walked to her locally made hatchback and drove herself. The other mums looked on in horror too as their imported, chauffeur-driven SUVs pulled up. The Dotwallas must have fallen on very bad times indeed.

Lesson Three
Home Science

From: Ambika S <Ambika.s@cvs.in>
To: Grade III B Parents Group
Date: 22 Mar 2022 at 9:52 PM
Sub: Addendum to Orientation

Dear Parents,

I'm so sorry I forgot to discuss a few points in the orientation.

- Students to carry a home notebook tomorrow for rough work
- All books and bottles to be labelled
- IMPORTANT: Please send a family photograph for an activity tomorrow in 4X6 dimension

Once again, I look forward to meeting the children tomorrow.

Regards,
Ambika S.
Class Teacher, III B

From: Ambika S <Ambika.s@cvs.in>
To: Grade III B Parents Group
Date: 22 Mar 2022 at 9:55 PM
Sub: Addendum to Addendum

Please note: No fancy stationery or bottles or tiffin boxes allowed in school.

Regards,
Ambika S.
Class Teacher, III B
From: Ambika S <Ambika.s@cvs.in>

To: Grade III B Parents Group
Date: 22 Mar 2022 at 9:57 PM
Sub: Re: Addendum to Addendum

No junk except on Wednesdays.

Regards,
Ambika S.
Class Teacher, III B

From: Ambika S <Ambika.s@cvs.in>
To: Grade III B Parents Group
Date: 22 Mar 2022 at 9:58 PM
Sub: Re: Re: Addendum to Addendum

Please read that as no junk FOOD except on Wednesdays.

Regards,
Ambika S.
Class Teacher, III B

Giselle

Time: 10.32 p.m.
Unread emails (478)

FFS! Home is where the heart is? Home is where the *heat* is!

The day was a disaster! We've had three refusals for the Bathware position and if we don't deliver a candidate in another two weeks, we will lose exclusivity of the contract. Nobody wanted the shitty job. I was so agitated, I even ended up logging into those ridiculous portals to look for suitable résumés. But none of the profiles showcased risk-taking ability. The only one willing to take risks was apparently the landlord of my office building, who turned up with a pest-control team and asked everyone to vacate the premises. I glared at him till he shrunk visibly but I had to leave anyway. I did suggest we wear masks and continue, but Vinti, who heads HR, told me we're an audited company and it's a safety hazard. Besides, it's 6 p.m. anyway, she argued. I don't even know what that meant!

So, I was back at home, in fucking daylight, and Kevin was so stunned to see me, he was speechless.

'Is it your half day?' he asked as I pushed past him.

'Why are you here?' I asked him. 'Don't you have swimming class?'

'Done.'

'Soccer?'

'Done.'

'Art?'

'Doesn't happen today.'

'Music?'

'Guitar or tabla?'

'Guitar.'

'Done. Before you ask, tabla doesn't happen today.'

'So why aren't you with Aryan?'

'Because we have school tomorrow, and Pareeta Aunty said Aryan has to eat and sleep on time.'

Man, Pareeta ran a tight ship.

'Okay, I'll be in my office if you need anything,' I announced opening the door to my home office, where, surprise, surprise, Rajiv seemed to be occupying the chair.

'What are you doing here?' I asked.

'I had a meeting in Gurgaon. You?'

'There's pest control happening at the building.'

'So they got rid of their biggest pest?'

Rajiv and his sense of humour. 'Where am I supposed to work, then? Why didn't you tell me you're going to be home?' I snapped.

'You didn't tell me you're going to be home either. Now if you can excuse me, I have a call to make.'

I let out a string of expletives as I shut the door behind me and found Kevin watching me, his mouth hanging open.

'Mama, you said the F word.'

'Because I'm forty.'

'You're thirty-eight.'

'You can say it when you're thirty-eight too.'

He pouted as I brushed past him to the bedroom to set up my workstation. I was ten minutes in when I was quaked by the cries of 'yee-haw' emerging from the adjacent room. I wouldn't be surprised if Clint Eastwood himself had descended on a brown stallion, doing a rodeo. The tenth yee-haw was even louder, so I stomped out of the room and there he was, my offspring, wearing a gigantic straw hat, riding his ridiculously expensive, stupid stuffed toy horse.

I called out to the nanny and asked her to keep it down to which she cowered in the corner. I sat down again, slamming the door behind me to make my point for my need of silence, and began work on the search again.

Kevin's head popped into my room and I almost cried in frustration. 'Not now, baby.'

'My horse stopped working.'

Thank the good lord! 'We'll fix it after dinner.'

Grumbling, he left the room. 'Shut the door!' I yelled.

I turned back to my work but two minutes later, Kevin's little round face appeared by my side again.

'What should I play with then?'

'What? Why do I have to decide? Play with your Lego. Play with your cars. Do anything! Just get out of my ... Just go, Kev. Please. I really have to finish this!'

'Can I get screen time?'

'No.'

Exactly three minutes later, he was at the door again.

'It's not me this time!' he yelped putting up his hands in surrender. 'Didi wants to know what to cook for dinner.'

Why was this my job! Why? I was one of the three people who ate dinner in this house. Why did I have the honour of deciding the fucking menu for all three people?

'Tell her to ask Daddy.'

He relayed it to her and then, no surprises there, reappeared. 'She's saying she can't ask him because he's working.'

'And what am I doing, Kevin? Am I dancing?'

Kevin giggled. 'Is that how you dance?'

I stood up, picked up my laptop and marched to the office room. 'Get out!' I told Rajiv even though he was on a conference call. 'Get out; I want my room.'

Rajiv rolled his eyes and walked out, still on the phone. I turned to Kevin and shot him a warning look. 'I don't want to be disturbed, okay? Pretend I'm not here.'

'Great! Then I'll just watch TV,' he said gleefully. I wanted to stop him but also needed peace.

When I emerged at half past ten, depleted of any energy, Rajiv was at the dining table, eating a salad. He pushed a bowl towards me.

'Long day?' he asked.

'As always.'

'Sorry to make it longer, but we have to send in a 4X6 picture to school tomorrow.'

I stopped chewing. 'And you're telling me this at 10.30 at night?'

'The email just came an hour ago.'

FFS! Was there nothing Rajiv could do without me?

Jia

Your friend Riddhi messaged. Rabia has to take a 4 X 6 picture for class tomorrow

What? When did they say that?

She's saying some email came in

Wait, I'll just check

Yes there's an email.

What a scatterbrained teacher!

She could've told us this morning!

So will you get home and do it?

If that's your way of finding out whether I'm on my way home then yes I am, Mother India

Don't text and drive

I'm in an Uber

> Where's your car?

I didn't take it

Because of the orientation

Is Rabia asleep?

> Brushed, bathed, tucked in

Yes, but is she asleep?

> Not a wink

I'll be home in ten

Don't let her sleep. We'll take a selfie and print it out

And you better not sleep too

> Why?

You need to be in the picture?

> It's a family picture!

You're her family

> I'm not her mother

You're her grandmother. Just don't let her sleep, ok?

Kainaz

	A chronological list of how the first day of school looked:
1.	4.00 a.m.: Woke up in anticipation of that alarm for 6.00 a.m. would not go off and that we'd miss the first day of school.
2.	5.00 a.m.: Rechecked all alarms and tried to meditate self back to sleep.
3.	5.30 a.m.: Got out of bed. Waiting for sleep to arrive was futile. Prepared tiffin.
4.	6.00 a.m.: Alarm went off on five devices, including Alexa that I was pretty sure I hadn't set. The internet is always listening.
5.	6.10 a.m.: Pondered ...
6.	6.30 a.m.: Woke up Ahaan with a big hug and pep talk. He was too sleepy to process anything.
7.	7.00 a.m.: Got him ready. T-shirt and shorts. Wanted to cry at the casualness of the uniform. He had a striped shirt and a striped tie back in St. Jon's.
8.	7.05 a.m.: Checked bag against checklist from orientation to ensure he was carrying all the necessary stationery.
9.	7.10 a.m.: Ahaan watched me strangely. Gave him another big hug. Kids are so transparent about their feelings. I hoped he didn't know how I felt, though they

	know. They always know. Which is why he kept looking at me questioningly.
10.	7.15 a.m.: Turned out the question was why I wasn't giving him breakfast. Between tiffin, uniform and ridiculously long hugs, I'd forgotten all about feeding my child.
11.	7.18 a.m.: Shoved cereal down Ahaan's throat as I asked Varaz to wake up and make him toast.
12.	7.20 a.m.: Ran to the bus stop, only to realize we'd forgotten his bottle at home.
13.	7.24 a.m.: Got glared at by several parents for holding up the bus while Varaz went running to fetch the bottle. When they saw him, their anger melted. It cost us three selfies later.
14.	7.35 a.m.: Told Varaz I had no idea *We Are the Gondals* had been so popular in the north. He claimed to not know either.
15.	8.15 a.m.: Collapsed with my iPad and sketched myself a trophy of Worst Mum of the Year Award.
16.	9.00 a.m.: Varaz kissed me goodbye and left for the office.
17.	9.05 a.m.: Cried remembering Goa.
18.	9.15 a.m.: Realized I had to send a 4X6 family photo to school that I had totally forgotten about.
19.	10.00 a.m.: Found one from our farewell party in Goa. Cut out cousin and her husband, and sent it to school through Swiggy.
20.	10.05 a.m.: Bit into the most tasteless banana for breakfast.
21.	10.10 a.m.: Cried about Goa.

Riddhi

Weight: 71.8 kgs
Diet Plan: Bran and oats with green, leafy vegetables

I had a bite of Lay's Potato Chip. Mummy looked at me strangely, but I told her potatoes have leaves and I had to have green 'leafy' vegetables. Also, it was from the green packet, not yellow or red or blue that they call Magic Masala when the only magic is that you turn blue yourself wanting water because of the mirchi. But Shivam toh eats full-full packets of the blue Lay's as if he was born with Dermi Cool thanda-thanda-cool-cool powder in mouth and like he didn't feel any mirchi only. But if I put even a pinch of mirchi in his dal he will act like he needs the fire brigade!

Anyway, I was looking through old photos. Syra had taken out so many albums yesterday for some activity at school—I didn't know what because she only checks my email half the time but she jumped out of bed at 10 p.m. because crazy teacher had sent the email so late.

I tried to tell her to take photos from all our trips abroad since background and all looks nice but she said who cares about the background. It should show family is true spirit. She picked one from Manali, but I said no because I was carrying Shivam at that time. Because he was refusing to be in pram. Then she picked one from Dubai where I looked lovely inside Burj Khalifa, but Harsh is looking like an Archies shop teddy bear. He was so chubby then. I told her to take one from Eiffel Tower trip but she said we cannot be seen in it, only tower. Then the one where we are leaning like Leaning Tower of Pizza but she said it wasn't normal enough. As if we were normal! Anyway, she chose one from SIL's Diwali party last year but my hair wasn't blow dried so I said no. So finally she took one from Shivam's birthday party last year. I told her Gudiya, cake cannot be seen in photo and I'd spent ten thou on it but she looked at me like I was mad. Which seven-year-old gives mother that look!

But see how smart I am? I always keep print out of photos. Harsh always made fun of me for wanting to print, but I love photo albums! Every holiday even now I come back, and send photos to Bhaiya's Kodak shop in Naraina main market and get album made. And look how useful it is now! Syra could just take photo out and go to school!

I wondered what Jia had done. Had she sent photo of just her and Rabia or one with her stupid husband also? I couldn't ask. She was my BFF but I didn't want to ask.

I was sure Rekha Tandon sindoorwali must have sent photo of their London house. She's very smart. Always wants teacher to know how she has summer home in London. Even puts on English accent every now and then. 'Would you like some tea?' Are we still in British Raj or what?

Anyway, I'm also sure Giselle Savarkar wouldn't have sent any photo at all. She is so lost. Always asking for homework on the group. Why she can't open school portal herself?

I sat around for fifteen minutes looking through albums, getting nostalgic. Then I picked up phone and messaged Jia to ask what she sent. Curiosity may have killed the cat, they say, na, but not Riddhi Makheeja Chhabra. As always, Jia was too busy to respond.

Lesson Four

Communication & Technology

From: Ambika S <Ambika.s@cvs.in>
To: III B Parents Group
Date: 1 May 2022 at 3:31 PM
Sub: Reg. Communication

Dear Parents,

Every Child is a different flower and together they make a beautiful garden.

It has been an exciting one month of having the children back in their classrooms. Thank you for your cooperation in settling them in.

We have been receiving a lot of emails and notes in the diaries. Some points regarding the same:

- Kindly note that only important information needs to be passed on to the teachers. Some of you have made beautiful videos of your Easter break but we're not sure how it's relevant to the class.
- Teachers will take forty-eight hours to respond to your email. A response during school hours is impossible and even after school hours, there is an expected turnaround time. Please do not send five follow up emails within forty-eight hours asking if we've seen the email.
- Emails regarding last-minute changes of mode of transport will not be accommodated. Also, requesting parents who come by car for pick up to kindly collect their children on time and not send emails saying 'running late by 10 mins' and turning up thirty minutes later.

- Tiffin boxes, bottles, forgotten notebooks, stationery cannot be sent via Dunzo/Swiggy/Zomato to school. Please teach your child a sense of responsibility by letting them carry things themselves.

In case of any emergency, kindly contact the school on 0124-444333.

Regards,

Ambika S.
Class Teacher, III B

Ambika

I am beginning to think that Grade Coordinator Shilpa Anand isn't her happiest with me. Once again she was at my desk chewing down her nails like an explosive was about to go off on her head.

'Oh no! Oh no!' she kept saying as she went through the email I'd sent out. She called in Sahiba to show me the beautiful email she had sent on communication rules.

> Mine: Every Child is a different flower and together they make a beautiful garden.
> Sahiba's: *'Good words are worth much, and cost little.'*— Unknown

'You see?' Shilpa Anand said. 'This quote is not only relevant, it's in quotes. Yours has no context, and that's plagiarism there unless you mention the source and put it in quotes.'

Like, which of these snooty parents even had the time to sue me for plagiarism? And what is the point of attributing it to an unknown author? At least I'd put in a quote after the last time when she'd erupted like Mount Vesuvius. She'd made such a big example of me at the previous teacher training.

Plus, who would even sue me? Half of them plagiarized the assignments they clearly did for their children!

'And this,' Shilpa continued.

> Mine: Kindly note that only important information needs to be passed on to the teachers. Some of you have made beautiful videos of your Easter break but we're not sure how it's relevant to the class.
> Sahiba's: Thank you for constantly communicating with us and keeping us abreast of the developments in your child's journey. We are so pleased that you consider us worthy partners.

'We *want* them to continue communicating with us!' Shilpa Anand said.

I certainly did not! I would be happier with fewer and shorter emails. Just bullet points would suffice. I wanted to say that but she was back to cross-referencing my email.

'And the tone, Miss Ambika! The tone!'

I wanted to tell her to watch hers. She sounded tearful. She rubbed her face and thanked Sahiba for joining us. Sahiba gave me a small sympathetic smile and left. I took that as encouragement and pulled the chair closer, turning the screen towards me.

'Yes, but look at this, Shilpa!' I caught her astonishment in time. 'Er, Miss. I mean, Miss Shilpa ... Anand. Look at some of these ridiculous emails I receive from parents every single day!'

> Dear Miss Ambika, Aanya didn't eat her tiffin today. Why?

'Because Aanya got a broccoli parantha! Can you imagine that? I mean, getting greens in whatever way is great, but *broccoli*? How do you even mince broccoli?' I argued.

'I have children, Miss Ambika, and broccoli has multiple health benefits,' Shilpa Anand said defensively. 'You can just boil and mash the broccoli, and the child wouldn't know. Besides, look at your response! "Try sending something tastier." How can you even say that?'

'Look at this one,' I said turning her attention to another gem.

> Dear Miss Ambika, Vidyut said he didn't do susu in school today.

'Like, why is his bathroom schedule *my* responsibility?'

'But, as a parent, Miss Ambika, using the washroom is important for the children,' Shilpa Anand defended the parents again. 'And why have you responded with "Tell him to drink more water"? Miss Ambika, you should encourage bathroom breaks. You should make the parent feel heard. You can't pass it back to them.'

I was beginning to notice a pattern here. She was on the parents' side, probably because she hadn't encountered the maniacs I had.

'Okay, how about this?

> Miss Ambika, Adarsh was bullying my son today. He pushed him and my son was hurt! I want to escalate this matter to Mrs Mehta!

'And this is not bullying, Shilpa! It was just an accident! I told the parent just as much.'

'Oh my god, Miss Ambika! You've actually said, "overreacting much"? In the response? Overreacting much? *Overreacting much?*'

See? Now she was overreacting much!

'There are many children who could accuse her son of the same,' I said trying not to roll my eyes. 'Anyway, read this one:

> Miss Ma'am, Humaira called my daughter bitch today. Is this the language we're teaching them?

Shilpa Anand gasped. 'That is appalling! We can't have our children using such language! Why haven't you raised this in our weekly meetings?'

'Yes, but we're not the ones teaching it. You're missing the point! It's not like we have a class dedicated to swear words and violence! No, wait, one more. This one emails me a lot!

> Miss Ambika, why wasn't my child included in the morning prayer team today? He loves to sing.

'How lovely!' Shilpa Anand said annoyingly. 'We must take note and include the child.'

'Well, according to the parent, the child is a star at everything! He sounds like nails on a chalkboard. Read these:

> Miss Ambika, Tania does not eat her banana.
> *It's rotten!*
> Miss Ambika, Kiera's black pencil is missing.
> *So get her another one!*

> Miss Ambika, My son has fever today. Please make sure he rests in school today!
> *Why is the child even in school?*

Shilpa Anand bit her lip. 'But, Miss Ambika,' she pleaded, 'they're parents!'

I inhaled deeply. 'Yes! Exactly! So why are they behaving like children?'

Shilpa Anand shook her head in disappointment. 'Remember, Miss Ambika. The parents are always right.' With that she stood up. 'I don't know. Maybe ... Maybe we need to schedule another training for you.'

'For me? What about the parents?'

'Oh, Miss Ambika! Let me send you a few articles from Teaching Inc. and we'll discuss this again, okay?'

'But I don't get it,' I argued. 'They all seem like these well-educated, smart, well-turned out, posh people but they have no manners. Have you seen the clothes they wear? The cars they drive? The lifestyles they lead? But when it comes to school, they treat us like their personal staff!'

'That's not true! They're very respectful.'

'Only to our face! You're criticizing my tone in the emails, look at theirs!'

She sighed loudly. 'They're *parents*! Their children mean the world to them. They want the best for them. They come to CVS for just that nurturing. And look at how you're talking to them. I think you should cut them some slack. They lead hard lives.'

Hard lives? It must be tough to go to the spa every day or, you know, find a tutor for your child or instruct the help to make tiffin boxes or, you know, land up in their fancy offices and get paid lakhs of rupees. I, on the other hand, ran a house on a paltry salary, wore the same outfit twice a week, worked eight-hour days and managed help who turned up only on salary day. And I had to have patience with them?

Shilpa Anand left the room and I picked up my phone to message Dodo.

> See if this email reads rude.

I forwarded the communication rules email to him and received a response in five minutes.

> Very!

Dammit, nobody was on my side!

Till now, I thought this job wasn't right for me because of the annoying children. Apparently, the job wasn't right because of the annoying parents.

Giselle

Time: 2.30 p.m.
Unread emails (999)

Shit hit the ceiling!
There was no one to pick up Kevin from the bus stop today. No one! The nanny packed up and left. Nobody knows why. Rajiv tried to put the blame on me but I flipped it right back at him. So he did what he does best. He left. Not left me; just left for the airport. He had a flight to catch.

Anyway, there was no one to fall back on—the driver went off with the Gates Foundation paperwork, Kitty from my team was on maternity leave and Silky, the new girl, blinked at me and responded with, 'But I'm from IIM. You can't possibly be expecting me to go fetch your son from the bus stop.' She was so damn rude! I wrote to my HR that this insubordination must go in her permanent file, but Vinti hit me with the audited company shit again. I bloody own the company but am not allowed to make my own rules!

I thought I'd write to Kevin's teacher to let him get off the bus unsupervised, then I remembered we had got this rude email from her on communication last week so it looked like she was on her own trip.

I called Pareeta to help, but she was at some ultrasound appointment. She had been looking bloated of late but I had thought it was all her baking making her fat.

'So ask your maids to fetch Kevin too,' I said.

'The girls are on leave today.'

'Both of them? How can you give them the day off together?' I cried.

She said it didn't matter. It didn't matter! Really! Pareeta lived in some fantastical universe clearly where fairies turned up to magically do the household chores. Mine looked hit by a hurricane today. We'd just about managed to get Kevin dressed in time; I'd thrown in a packet of chips for lunch, Rajiv had run out to drop him to the bus stop, calling me twice to find out where the bus stop was located and then I had rushed to office without a thing in my stomach. And here, Pareeta was acting like Mother Teresa herself, an epitome of calm and generosity, giving both her girls leave on the day I needed them the most!

'Who's fetching Aryan and Vidya from the bus stop?'

'My mother is, but you'll have to coordinate with her directly. I'm lying down on the ultrasound table now and the technician doesn't seem very happy.'

'I'm not a technician, I'm a doctor,' I heard someone say in the background before the line went dead.

Damn, I realized I should have enquired about her health first. Or taken her mother's number. I knew she stayed in the same society, but I had no idea which tower she stayed in. You needed a family/relative close by if you were going to single-handedly raise your kids like Pareeta was doing. I hadn't seen her husband in years. Maybe he was a figment of her imagination.

Anyway, I was stuck. Someone had to pick up the outcome of my sex life from the bus stop and, much like the Bathware position search, this was also fruitless. I glared at Silky, the 'IIM' babe, through my glass cabin and she stared coldly right back, so I left for the bus stop myself. In the middle of the fucking workday!

And there was not a person at the pick-up spot. Apparently, I was half an hour early. The timings had changed two years ago when they had moved from elementary to primary. And I didn't even care to remember!

I found myself a bench in the shade and sat down, taking out my phone to work. As luck would have it, the battery breathed its last within five minutes. I had nothing I could do except idle away time. I took off my shoes and rubbed the soles of my feet. They were killing me. Why? Because I'd been on my feet since 6.30 a.m. completing all the household chores. Why was I doing household chores? Because my house help had left. Which meant I had to find a new one. Mind maps.

I decided to use this time productively and poach a new nanny for Kevin. Especially now, as a lot of them were congregating to pick up the children. I studied them, trying to judge which one looked the smartest or the easiest to lure, but they all categorically avoided my eye.

Maybe Rajiv was right. Maybe I was building a reputation. Three house helps in six months. Eight, if you counted the ones who lasted less than a day. I needed someone to stick this time. Salary was not an issue, but they needed to have a certain amount of drive.

I started looking at the ones walking down the street, riding their cycles, walking in groups, in a hurry, busy, with little wallets in their hands, hitched up sarees, knotted dupattas. Who were the ones who looked like they had ambition? All of them, I guessed.

Suddenly, my eyes fell upon a reasonable-looking candidate; neat and well turned out, holding up an umbrella and carrying a basket of vegetables.

'Oye! Hello!'

The girl looked up at me and she looked vaguely familiar. I wondered if she'd worked for me earlier.

'Were you talking to me?' she responded.

I was shocked! Thank god I hadn't called her 'Didi' or 'Aunty' or whatever else we call our staff. It seemed to be someone I knew. A resident perhaps?

'Helloo …' I said with caution.

She looked at me confused. Maybe she didn't know me. Maybe I was mistaken. Then she smiled back.

'Hi, I'm so sorry. I know I met you at Ahaan's orientation, but I'm still trying to remember all the names.'

Fuck! She was a parent from Kevin's class! She wasn't a maid! Fuck! Fuck! Fuckity! Fuck!

I gathered my wits. 'Yes, of course. I'm Giselle, Kevin's mum. You looked familiar.'

'I'm Kainaz.'

'Right. Are you carrying … vegetables?'

'Fruit.'

'Of course.' None of that produce looked recognizable. Not like I'd know. What on earth was that strange-looking stuff in her basket? 'I didn't know you lived here.'

'I don't. I live in Travancore Estate.'

'Travancore Estate? But that's way down the road. What are you doing here?'

'Uh ... someone told me you get a better variety of fruit at this ... shop or whatever it's called ... Mandi ... At this mandi.'

'So you *walked all the way*?' I know I didn't have to enunciate it like that, but it was forty degrees in the sun, for crying out loud, and to walk all the way for *fruit*?

'Um ... yes. And I'm glad I did. It had really good quality fruit.'

'Right.' I looked away, trying to think of a way to end this conversation. 'Okay, then, I'll see you around.'

She looked a bit surprised at—what does Rajiv say it is?—my brazen-ness but she nodded politely and walked away.

That's when it struck me. She was the new mum! The one with the celebrity husband! And who Pareeta said had fallen on hard times. The husband had been on a daily soap at some point in time and was very popular ... I think I even Googled him.

Oh well, whose life wasn't a daily soap, anyway.

Pareeta

Week 10

'Is it safe?'

I stopped whipping the cream and looked at my mother. She sat there, helping me decorate the macaroon tower, her glasses at the edge of her nose. I swallowed.

'Dr Thukral says it is.'

'And you're sure you want to go ahead with it? I mean, it won't be easy to change your mind after this.'

'Yes,' I said firmly.

'Maybe I'll speak to Sambhavi myself, if that's okay with you?'

'No, Mama, it doesn't concern you and you can't just talk to my gynaec because she's your friend,' I said putting down the cream and taking a seat.

'You're forty-two, Pareeta.'

'I know that. Dr Thukral said that as long as we get regular scans and I stay active, it will be all right.'

'And Pankaj is okay with this?'

My heart started racing and I couldn't look my mother in the eye. 'Are you sure?' had been his question every single time. 'We already have a complete family, and at this age and this juncture of your career …'

How much our careers meant to us! The first pregnancy that we lost because we were too early in our careers. Then Vidya happened and we didn't want another one for seven more years because we were still unstable in our careers. And now this long-distance marriage for the sake of our careers. *His* career.

'Well?' Mama prodded.

'He's fine. Now can we stop talking about it? I haven't told Aryan.'

'You should tell him.'

'I will in good time.'

'This is a good time.'

Aryan came bursting into the room with Kevin and I shot a warning look at Mama.

'You won't believe what happened in school today!' Aryan said bursting into giggles. 'Chirag farted!' He began laughing hysterically.

'Pareeta Aunty, it was so funny! We were doing an experiment on the properties of air and we had to blow a balloon, and Chirag blew so hard, he *farted*!'

Aryan and Kevin both doubled over with laughter and I told them it wasn't a nice thing to do. It must've been embarrassing for him.

'No, it wasn't!' Kevin argued. 'He laughed himself! And so did Miss Ambika!'

'Oh my god! Even Miss Ambika! That's not nice!' I gasped.

'Everyone did, except Syra. She said it's a normal body function and she finds nothing funny about it.'

Always so wise. 'I agree with Syra. I'm surprised at your teacher.'

Realizing he wasn't getting any laughs from me, Aryan changed the subject. 'Where were you anyway? Did you get me anything?'

'I was at the doctor,' I said absent-mindedly.

'Doctor? Why?' Aryan asked in alarm. I saw Vidya watching me.

I cleared my throat. 'It's all fine. I was just feeling a little unwell. But I'm okay.'

'Just have a Dolo, Aunty P,' Kevin suggested. 'That's what my Mama has. She says Daddy gives her a headache. And Daddy says she gets a headache every night.'

God, Giselle really needs to watch what she says in front of her kid!

Lesson Five
Economics

From: Ambika S <Ambika.s@cvs.in>
To: III B Parents Group
Date: 12 May 2022 at 5:35 PM
Sub: Fwd: Summer Break

Dear Parents,

>> *'Life is better in flip-flops. And even better in summer vacations.'*—Unknown

>> We're delighted that our summer break is starting from 16 May to 3 July.

>> The holiday homework is attached with this email. Do utilize this break to refamiliarize your children with academic concepts and help them work creatively on defined projects.

>> We also urge you to use this time to enjoy new experiences, develop familial bonds and create new memories.

>> We would like to take this opportunity to discuss a matter of utmost importance: Birthday parties—many of which will be celebrated over the break. Kindly bear in mind the CVS policy of simplicity:
- Handmade gifts and return gifts are encouraged
- Only send e-invites
- Please use recyclable décor
- We encourage homemade healthy food at birthday parties
- Only frosting-free cakes allowed for school celebrations, 1 kg only per child

>> Wishing you a restful holiday season.

>> Regards,
>> Shilpa Anand

Regards,
Ambika S.
Class Teacher, III B

Riddhi

Weight: 72.6 kgs
Diet Plan: Planned: Only proteins
Consumed: Only carbs

Uff! I love birthday parties! It has everything: socializing, good clothes, good food and, the best part—your children are someone else's headache.

Syra also loves birthday parties. She likes to come first in all games.

I have toh always been very social. I have school friends, college friends, colony friends, cousin friends, mummy friends, Harsh's friend group wife friends ... What is life without friends? I keep telling Syra but she only sticks to Rabia. Thank god she comes first in class so everyone wants to invite her, otherwise we would have no invites only. Even at all my birthdays, class topper Preeto Shekhawat would always be invited every time even though he was absolute bore. He only got interesting when he turned sixteen and went to jail. But by then we stopped having birthday parties.

Also, food at children birthday is best! Pizza, chowmein and fondant cake. If teacher, after sending all those rule email, was to see this now, she would faint. No rules were followed ever!

Nowadays birthday function outfits is becoming very trendy. Because of Insta, you can't repeat outfits. I get fresh clothes made from Dolly Aunty boutique just for birthday season. I can't wear heavy clothes like I have to wear at family kitty, na. I also have lovely dresses for Syra, but she says not to waste money and she can repeat. She is such a grandmother!

Anyway, this week was sindoorwali Rekha Tandon's son's birthday. I wore my yellow flower maxi dress with golden sandal and purple hairband, and carried my new Fendi bag (fresh fake from Bangkok—my SIL just went). It was a Transformers party and my Syra was fascinated by machines, so was just too excited.

I called Jia and told her I'd pick her up too. Jia toh you know acts like the office would fall and crumple if she didn't work. But I brainwashed her that she needs to act like true parent and take Rabia for birthday parties because what if they're stuck in India forever and never go back to US, then who will be Rabia's friends if she doesn't go for birthday parties? I think she just wanted me to stop talking so said okay-okay to coming. She said she'll get her own car but I've seen the maniac way she drives. Best if I picked her only.

So we went in my MG Gloster with one driver while nanny with children went in BMW with other driver—the drama one who wears helmet even in the car around Shivam just because he heard last driver had quit because Shivam threw bat at him. So Jia and I were peaceful, and had a nice chat on our way. Jia said something about how purpose of going with Rabia is defeated if we travel in different cars but I told her, Jia, they don't want to talk to

Mamas, they only want to see our face. Bas. It's like putting proxy attendance. But I think so she and Rabia share very unique bond. They always whispering and laughing and all that. Syra, on the other hand, only gives me gyaan.

'How is Mumma?' I asked Jia.

'She's fine,' she said sending emails on phone.

'And any update from police?'

'None.'

I sighed. 'Harsh sold a house to an SP last month, 60 per cent black. If you want, I can find out more.'

Jia reached out and squeezed my hand. 'It's okay. I'm tired of it anyway.'

I squeezed her hand back. I'm glad she didn't say find out because bhai, SP paying 60 per cent cash to buy a house would have asked for bribe to find out also. And Harsh toh is against bribe. Except when he has to bribe offices to get work done quickly. Or when he has to sell in black. Or during school admissions. Not ours of course! Syra is such a genius CVS took her in one go. But all nieces and nephews in Delhi, na, they need. Harsh is toh very generous.

'Did you see Miss Ambika's email?' I asked Jia. 'She didn't even bother to remove Shilpa Anand's name. Just forwarded email.'

'Who is Shilpa Anand?'

'Arrey, the grade coordinator. Don't you know? You need to be more involved mother. Why didn't Rabia come for Kushal's party?'

'Who Kushal?'

'Arrey, same whose father makes motorcycles.'

'I don't think we were invited.'

'How you can't be? I asked Madhvi also—Kushal's Mumma. She said she sent invite but you didn't respond.'

'I think we only get invited everywhere because of you.'

'Oh, shut up! Rabia is so popular also. Four parties I've attended since summers started. You should make more effort.'

Jia sighed and started looking at her phone again.

I looked out of the window as we entered Chhatarpur farms. Harsh has plot here and says we should move, but I say no, too much dark-dark and no road also. Like rollercoaster ride. Wonder how Varaz Dotwalla's wife will drive her small car here?

When we reached Rekha Tandon's house, uff! Transformer theme meaning transformation! Not only of house but also of Rekha Tandon. Such a short red dress she was wearing with such high heels and so much curls hair. If it wasn't for her sindoor, I would have never recognized her. Even sindoor was nice triangle shape today. She came and gave hug and air-kisses, and I also patted my freshly blow dried hair to show her. Then she introduced us to her husband, who acted like guest at his own party and ate starters before offering. Why fathers act like birthday party is only mother's job? Even Harsh tells me you only do party. And when bill comes, I tell him, now you do party!

I dumped children where games were happening with nanny, and went and sat under the garden umbrella. I pulled Jia to sit next to me and told her to switch off her phone—too much she works. Then I started checking out other mothers who came in.

Amrita–Amruta duo came together, obv. Amrita–Amruta have daughters called Kiera and Kaira, and they look ditto same, dress same and same amount they irritate also. I didn't like their outfits and I think so Amrita was carrying fake LV. I said so to Jia but she toh doesn't know brands only. Then

Pareeta came and I thought for a minute she was pregnant because her belly's become so big, but bakers are always round. Her Instagram page said she'd started baking sugar-free tea cakes so I ordered immediately. I ate one cake with tea in morning, one in afternoon tea, one with evening tea and one with after-dinner tea. Then dietician noted weight was 900 gm more and I thought hain, I ate only 800 gm cake so where other weight has come from? Must be water retention because of extra tea I had to have with the cake.

I told Pareeta her cakes were very nice and then also told her top wasn't suiting her, making her look preggers to which she blushed but I'm her friend, I should tell the truth. She should wear some asymmetrical suits like my Mausiji from Patiala. I tell you, so much nicer she looks now that she can hide her fat. Otherwise she looked stuffed like tandoori aloo. Now she has very modern-type bahu, who gave her makeover. Mummy accused Ginni, my bhabi, and said why my DIL couldn't give me makeover but I said to her, Mummy, thank your god. Have you seen Ginni's style sense? All the time, pink-pink. You want to look like talcum powder bottle or what?

I told Pareeta ki Pareetaji, no need to be pregnant—you have readymade third child. This Giselle forever sending her brat with Pareeta. Does he even go home? Pareeta laughed but she's such pleasant lady she always laughs.

Then Varaz Dotwalla's wife came in wearing capri and kurti, and I thought hai, wish her husband would have come instead, ankhein hi sek lete, but I still was polite.

'So, Kainazji, all settle in? Ahaan liking school? Found nanny?'

Her smile was little uncomfortable but she said they don't need nanny. I don't know how poor these people have become! If I didn't have nanny for my Shivam, I would be in Agra ka pagal khaana by now.

'So, everybody, what plans for the summer holidays?' Amrita–Amruta asked.

Only people who have plans themselves ask others. So that people ask them and they can boast. But I didn't ask. I launched into my itinerary for next six weeks and didn't give them chance to speak!

Kainaz

	How to throw a party at CVS:
1.	Select a venue that you would typically select for a wedding : They cannot be hosted at home. A banquet hall, a cinema theatre, a football field, a farmhouse. It should be able to accommodate three hundred people at least. And you must specify that it's a close family and friends thing.
2.	Select a theme that cannot be missed: Everything has to fall in line—décor, entertainment, return presents. Ahaan just won himself a Transformer iPad cover. He doesn't even own an iPad. Last week, we went for a birthday with a Wimpy Kid theme. The birthday boy did a great job of living up to the name.
3.	Decide on entertainment: Today's party had a large screen showing the movie in a corner and an even larger Transformer character moving around greeting everyone. Every now and then, some sort of scary character would walk past us, breathing out fire ... And the strangest thing of all? Nobody seemed to notice! That is the definition of entertainment now. So obscene that you wouldn't bat an eyelid.
4.	Have a celebrity caterer: You should be able to take a bite of the food and declare the name of the caterer.

> They served sushi at the previous party. Ahaan had taken one look and asked, 'Why are we eating koala food, Mama?' And of course, all parties had various versions of a margherita pizza—even though I didn't know there could be versions of it—but nowhere had I seen anything homemade
>
> 5. Get a cake that puts wedding cakes to shame: I really hoped nobody would burst out of the one that Rekha Tandon was wheeling in. It could not even be carried out. And the last one had six layers—every layer a different flavour.

I mean, honestly, it was all great. As long as Ahaan had no such expectations for his birthday. Presently, Riddhi pulled out her phone and took a selfie with the humongous cake. 'I need ideas, na. My Shivam turns five next to next to next month.'

The lady called Jia caught my eye and winked. I felt very comforted by that.

'Champion Valley birthday parties are really a bit too much,' Jia says leaning in. 'It's like having to plan a wedding.'

I smiled at her and she squeezed my hand.

There was something nice about her. You would think otherwise, given how stylishly she dressed and the amount of make-up she wore—she looked a tad bit intimidating. But Riddhi spoke of her a lot and perhaps the fact that she was a single mum, recently returned from the US, made me a wee bit warmer towards her. Perhaps she too was as appalled as I was by the pomp and show. Before I could ask her, Riddhi turned to me.

'You must be used to such parties, Kainazji. Mr Varaz being star and all. Have you met Shah Rukh Khan?'

Thank god, she didn't wait for an answer. For she was frowning now at Pareeta. 'What happened, Pareetaji? You look yellow.'

Pareeta

Week 12

I think she meant pale. I tried to smile, but I had a cramp. I told her as much. These long hours of standing in the kitchen to fulfil orders were beginning to take a toll on me. I perhaps needed to fix a higher chair where I could sit and work.

But Riddhi misunderstood, and asked someone to bring me a glass of Limca with heeng, ajwain and kala namak. It smelled as toxic as it sounded. I told her the cramp was in my leg, not in my stomach, but she refused to listen and insisted I take a sip.

'It's my Dadi's recipe. Few sips and you'll get a nice burp. Do you know how much rubbish my Shivam eats in a day? But not one stomachache. Just this mixture and it's all fine. Yes, farts are a little stinky, but at least no cramp.'

I took a whiff of the concoction and wanted to throw up. 'It's … I can't,' I said as politely as I could.

Jia wrinkled her nose. 'Oh god, Riddhi. It's vile!'

'No, it's Limca. It's also excellent for weight loss!' Riddhi announced.

I couldn't help but laugh. I reached out and squeezed her hand. For someone who had been on a diet ever since I'd known her, I wasn't sure I should take her word for it.

'Arrey, trust me, Pareetaji. Have a sip!'

I held my breath and took a sip so as to not hurt her feelings as she watched me expectantly.

'Dekha? You'll feel better very soon! Anyway, as I was saying, I am off to Abu Dhabi next week. Nobody goes to Dubai anymore. Too much commercial. Then we go to Poland, Iceland and Scandinaval. What about you, Pareetaji?'

I tried to ignore the cramp and not to laugh at 'Scandinaval'. 'I'm going to Mussoorie.'

'Oh lovely,' Jia exclaimed. 'How long?'

'For a month.'

'One full month!'

'Yes. We typically do the hills, take a cottage and stay there.'

'I can never stay in cottage. I need room service!' Riddhi looked like she had room service even at home.

'Rabia told me their class teacher was going to Mussoorie too,' Jia said. 'Maybe you'll bump into her.'

Oh, I hoped not. My Mussoorie holiday was always a large family affair. Cousins and their families, kids and spouses. Of course, Pankaj had missed the last three, which made me a bit sad again. But the kids looked forward to it and didn't mind the walk down Mall Road for entertainment every evening.

'And you, Kainazji?' Riddhi asked.

'Just the usual. Goa for a bit. Then my mum comes here.'

She always looked a bit sad, this Kainaz Dotwalla. 'Why just for a bit?' I asked.

'I need to be here. I'm setting up my business.'

'Achha! What business?' Riddhi prodded innocently, glancing at me. I knew she was trying to get at.

'Furniture,' Kainaz said nonchalantly. 'Like I said, I'm a carpenter.'

I mean, it was strange. When she'd said it the first time, we thought we'd misunderstood what she was trying to say.

'So you'll have a team working with you?' I asked helpfully.

'No, I do the woodwork myself. I've found a place in Sikanderpur and I have a few suppliers.'

'So they'll supply the furniture,' Riddhi said helpfully.

'No, they'll supply the wood. I'll make the furniture.'

To be honest, I was a baker. I cooked food. I must look as odd as she looked to us.

'That's really interesting,' Jia said. 'It must be very fulfilling.'

'It is.' Kainaz was always so innocent.

'Hai, gareebi,' Riddhi whispered. Riddhi was always so crazy.

We sat a bit awkwardly then and concentrated on our food. Only Jia seemed unperturbed. But, then again, maybe because she wore so much makeup, I couldn't really tell her actual expression.

'Hey, Pari!' someone crooned from behind me. Turned out to be Anaaithhaa Kulkarni, one of the poshest mums in class, who clearly believed a lot in numerology. I cursed under my breath. I really did not want to do the sitting/standing bit again. My leg was really cramping up. Almost wincing, I stood up and she gave me an air kiss.

'Loved the fig cookies, Pari! You've outdone yourself!'

I squeezed her hand. 'So glad you liked it, Anaaithhaa.'

'I hope I'm seeing you at Kkaran's birthday next Saturday!'

'Aryan will be there, but I have a really large corporate order so may not be able to make it.'

'Oh no, darling; no excuses! You must be there! As must you, Riddhi.'

'Your friend's hotel again? Your farmhouse still not ready?' Riddhi asked, batting her eyelashes faux innocently.

'Oh, I'm so particular, darling. I keep sending things back because it's not good enough. The wood quality or the finishing …'

I glanced at Kainaz and decided to step in. 'Have you met our friend, Kainaz Dotwalla? She's a furniture stylist,' I offered.

Kainaz looked up shocked but introductions were quickly made.

'She's Varaz Dotwalla's wife,' I said because I knew, with someone like Anaaithhaa, name dropping would make all the difference. I could see her eyes light up.

'Oh, the actor! Of course, of course. I did not know you're into furniture! I'd love to connect. Listen, it's Kkaran's birthday next week. Why don't you join us? In fact, give me your number. I'll text you the invite right away.'

I saw Jia looking at her phone and felt embarrassed for her. She had not been invited even though she was right there. Not like she looked disturbed, honestly. But it was a bit of a trend among other mothers—this suspicion around her because she was single, a bit stand-offish and her make-up made her look a little … You know what I mean.

Then I saw Kainaz look at her phone and turn purple. Kkaran's birthday invitation had been WhatsApped to her, I guessed. It was a two-minute video, shot by a professional, a one-minute ode to Anaaithhaa's beloved son with the parents floating around in colour-coordinated outfits, running down castles and hills, and another minute of people gushing over his many wonderful qualities. It was the most extravagant invite I'd received, and I'd received many, trust me. I was told the family had especially taken a trip to Austria to shoot it.

It certainly wasn't easy being a CVS parent. There was always so much fabulousness to keep up with.

Lesson Six
Political Science

From: Rekha Tandon rekharocks@rst.com
To: III B Parents Group
Date: 10 July 2022 at 8:16 AM
Sub: PTA event

Hello fellow parents!

Welcome back from the summer hols!

As you would be aware, three parents from our class have joined the PTA this year—Girish Munjal, Riddhi Makheeja Chhabra and myself. We will be keeping you informed about the various activities and events being planned by the PTA executive body.

The school is in the process of upgrading their gym. As a gift from the PTA, we will be holding a bake sale in school every Friday so that we can raise funds for buying them some new equipment.

Our class, III B, will be responsible for the sale on 20 July. Request volunteers to man the stall as well as put their culinary skills to test.

Looking forward to generous participation.

Cheers!
Rekha Tandon
PTA Member, 2022-23

Jia

> Hello Jia! Wanted to personally request you to participate in the bake sale happening this Friday

> Who's this?

> Rekha Tandon, Aseer's mom

> You came for our birthday party in the summers

> At our Chhatarpur farm home

> Hello?

> Are you there?

> Yes. Hi

> Hi!

> So this is just a reminder to participate in the bake sale

> We need to showcase our class strength & our school spirit

> It's this Friday

> You can bake cookies, cakes, muffins, cupcakes, anything

> We are open to ideas

> Please do confirm

> Also the quantity

> Hello?

> Hello? Please respond

Sorry, I can't bake

> If you've seen my email, you can send any other eatables or drinks too

Which email? I have six of them from you

> Can I call? Easier to explain on the phone

Sorry, in a meeting

> You can send savouries like pizza, burgers, sandwiches or beverages like cold coffee, iced tea or milkshakes

> I'd like a confirmation on what you'll be sending

> I'm putting down the final list

> I'm sure you're really busy but can I put down sandwiches for you?

Cheese or lettuce tomato will do

Hello?

———•———

Jia, what u said to Rekha tandon? Shes so pissed

> Hi Riddhi

Arrey what u said na

> Nothing!

Exctly! She saying u nt respondng

> She was going on and on about the bake sale

I told her u bringng 10 pcks frooti

> I'm not

Ill send on ur behalf

> No you won't

U hv 2 do sum things 4 schl n 4 frnd

> Who friend?

Me. Im in PTA

> Why are you in the PTA Riddhi?

> Coz Harsh said 2 me 2 enroll n b involved in schl affair

> U shd also join

> No thanks!

> Ok. Actly gd idea. Its v bore. So u will send?

> What?

> 10 pcks frooti

> No

> Mother India, can you get 10 packets of Frooti?

> What are we celebrating?

> Nothing. I need to send it for some PTA event

> Look at you! A PTA mom!

> Riddhi's coercing me!

> I find that hard to believe!

> LOL!

> LOL!

> Thanks Mom! <3

Kainaz

	A complete and comprehensive list of reasons I shouldn't be allowed near ovens:
1.	Because I don't know how to use them
2.	Because I don't know how to use them
3.	Because I don't know how to use them

Last night, I spent six hours baking cookies for the bake sale. I thought I would contribute positively towards the PTA event, in school spirit, and be seen as an active and involved parent—even though Varaz had looked at me doubtfully when I'd declared my intentions.

'But, K, you don't really bake.'

'Yes, but we've had an oven for years.'

'And never used it!'

'I've already asked Firdose for her famous cookie recipe, Varaz. It doesn't look very hard. By the way, would you know if baking powder and baking soda are the same thing?'

'I'll Google it ... No, apparently it's not. Hang on, I'll help you too. Where's my apron?'

We both started following the recipe Firdose had sent us, beating the eggs, measuring, whipping, mixing. Ahaan looked tempted to help but eventually sat down to draw a card for his friend Roshan's birthday back home. We listened to music, made a mess, it was a lovely evening.

'Did you get done with the signboard today?' Varaz asked me about my workshop.

'I did. Come in and see it tomorrow morning?'

I'd finally found a workshop and set it up last month in Sikanderpur. It was strange signing the lease because it was a market full of men and many had laughed openly in my face when I'd said I wanted to start my carpentry workshop. 'Warehouse', they'd corrected me, expecting me to be a reseller of sorts. 'Workshop', I'd clarified because I intended to make the pieces myself. Those who hadn't laughed had thought it as a rich girl's hobby, especially those who had met Varaz when he was accompanying me and asked him for an autograph. They'd immediately escalated the rentals when they saw a hint of celebrityhood, but then we'd met Mr Ghulam, who had very kindly given me his shop on the first floor at a reasonable rate and we'd signed the lease.

I never had to go through this drill back home. I used to make furniture in my backyard and sell as I pleased. But here, the houses were tiny and there were just so many rules!

Varaz and I had brainstormed on names for our shop. But it was my niece Naomi who had suggested I call it 'The Elder Wand'. She was going through a Harry Potter phase and could barely look up from her book to say it, but I thought it sounded positively magical. 'You're doing nothing short of magic anyway,' Varaz had said lovingly and so there I was, painting a signboard to be mounted in front of my shop.

I'd spent the whole day finalizing the design and painting, then gotten home in time to fetch Ahaan from the bus stop, helped him with his homework, prepared dinner—which I had to do myself since nobody here seemed to understand our cuisine and now here we were baking cookies.

When the first batch came out, they were underdone. So we put them back in again. Then they were overdone.

Varaz left to put Ahaan to bed, and I started measuring, whipping, beating yet again and put a third batch in. I obviously got something wrong because they looked like pieces of chunky cardboard.

When Varaz returned, we did the whole thing again and, by the time the clock struck midnight, we had our first batch of edible cookies, after five batches of failed ones, that were, yes, strangely shaped, but tasted pretty decent. Varaz and I both treated ourselves to one each.

'Not like Firdose's,' I admitted, 'but not bad either.'

'Maybe we can claim Ahaan baked them,' Varaz suggested. 'Then the imperfections are easier to overlook.'

I shook my head and reached for another cookie in dismay.

'Maybe we should have it with ice cream?'

'That's a great idea. Do we have some? I'll check.'

So we sat hunched over a bowl of vanilla with bits of crispy chocolate cookies. We chatted about this and that, about our friends in Goa, about how ridiculous the monsoons here looked in comparison, about Varaz's revived celebrity status and generally had a bit of a laugh. When we were done, Varaz offered to clear up while I went to pack the remaining cookies in butter paper. But something looked amiss.

'Varaz, how many did you have?'

'Two.'

'And I had two, but we only have six left. I'm pretty sure I baked twelve.'

'I had two too!' I heard a voice behind me. 'They're really good, Mama!'

'When did you get out of bed?'

'Just now only. I wanted to wish Roshan at twelve. Then we got chatting. The cookies were very good! But Aunty Firdose makes them better!' He waved and walked off innocently. I turned back to my cookies. I wondered if six made a good enough contribution for a bake sale.

Pareeta

Week 20

Of course I baked five types of cakes and they flew off the shelves within minutes at the PTA event. I had volunteered to do stall duty and Riddhi's eyes had popped out when I'd opened up the boxes.

'Hide these! Hide these, Pareetaji! I'll only buy it! Otherwise nothing will be left for me!'

I started to laugh just as Rekha Tandon shot her daggers with her eyes.

'We can't hide these!' she yelled, her skin turning the colour of her sindoor.

'But I'll pay for it! We'll raise money anyway. Full cake mine!' Riddhi said forcefully closing the lid on the chocolate one.

'Aren't you on a diet?' I asked.

'Bhaad mein gayi diet! You know what he's given me today? Tamatar only! ONLY! I've had tamatar toast for breakfast, tamatar shorba instead of tea, tamatar rice for lunch. I feel like I'm looking like tamatar. See? He gives me tamatar every two months. So annoying! Someone said tamatar not good for kidneys. I've been having pain all morning.' She clutched her side and I grew worried for a minute.

'That's because you slept on Shivam's gun, Ma,' Syra said from behind her, where she sat reading her book.

'Why aren't you in class?' Riddhi asked.

'Because Miss Ambika is on the PTA duty and I volunteered to help her. Pareeta Aunty, I'm sure your cakes will be gone in minutes. And our class will raise maximum money!'

I smiled at her as Rekha clapped her hands in glee. I glanced over at Miss Ambika, who was sitting in the corner scrolling on her phone. She looked like she could drop dead of boredom. Some school spirit that! I had tried to chat with her to gain some insight into Aryan's academic performance, but she'd just blinked at me and then glanced at my stomach. I felt very conscious, as if she knew, and moved away.

'No, Riddhi, you can't take the whole cake,' Rekha Tandon was arguing now as they held the box between them. 'I know you'll pay for it but we have to make sure our stall looks full.'

'It should look empty so that they know so much sale has happened!' Riddhi shot back, pulling the box back towards her.

I really hoped the cake wouldn't fall in the process. I looked at Syra for help but she simply grinned at me, clearly enjoying this burst of madness.

'Let it be!' Rekha said pulling it from one side just as Riddhi pulled it from the other. 'You let it be!'

Suddenly Miss Ambika emerged and pulled the box out of their hands.

'If you want the whole cake, please take it, Riddhi. The objective is to raise money anyway.' She placed it near Riddhi's bag and walked away.

'Dekha!' Riddhi said sticking her tongue out at Rekha.

Rekha pushed a perfectly curled tendril away from her face, almost smudging her famous sindoor. 'I don't know why she's authority here,' Rekha spat. 'She's the most incompetent teacher Aseer's everrrrr had. Hai na, Syra?'

Syra just shrugged. 'She's all right. Ma, you really shouldn't have the full cake.'

Rekha Tandon looked delighted. 'That's why your daughter's a genius!' she said pulling the box back and laying it out on display as the gates opened and parents started pouring in. Patting her hair, she looked ready to serve.

I touched Riddhi's shoulder sympathetically. 'I'll bake another low-cal one for you.'

'No,' Riddhi replied. 'Make a full fat one. What authority Rekha Tandon has over the teacher?'

'She's right though. This teacher's a bit ... weird,' I said making sure she couldn't hear us.

'No, she's not,' Syra said wisely. 'She's wonderful!'

For the first time, I doubted her wisdom.

Ambika

Syra was my little assistant. She rolled her eyes a lot at me and often walked up to the blackboard to correct my working or, embarrassingly, more often than not, my spellings, but I didn't mind it and neither did she. I always let her flip through the notebooks after I'd checked them so that she could point out any mistakes I'd made.

'Maybe you can grow up and become a teacher too,' I told her tapping her nose in appreciation.

She sighed. 'I'm going to be an astronaut, Miss Ambika. Teaching is not my ambition.'

'It's a great job. I get lots of holidays, and I work half days and I get to read books.' None of it was true. The summer vacations were a sham—I worked eight hours in school and twelve hours at home—and the only books I seemed to read were textbooks. But I wasn't going to be responsible for the disillusionment of a future potential educator—another precious term we were introduced to in our Vision for Children training.

Syra, of course, saw through me. 'Who are you trying to convince?'

'You also feel a bit like a celebrity,' I insisted. This bit was true, but, unfortunately, not in a positive way.

Sweet little Sahiba, class teacher III A, had warned me one afternoon when we were both eating our snacks in the staff room during a free period. She's been eyeing a particularly hot red dress on one of the shopping websites, when I was crossing her and I'd said it looked very becoming.

Now, typically, I didn't make any PC with the teachers. They felt alien to me. Especially when they shot me the same stunned/amused/disgusted look that Shilpa Anand particularly reserved for me, as if whatever I said seemed to scandalize them. But this Sahiba babe, who had been promoted from kindergarten teaching to primary, was all cherry-cheeked and angelic so I had warmed up to her.

Plus, I hadn't bought a dress for myself in what felt like ages. How easy it had been to like a dress and get it with a click. Now look at me, a pauper, living vicariously through other people's shopping escapades.

'I like the cut too,' I'd told her looking at the dress on her phone. 'You should buy it.'

She'd sighed. 'You know we can't wear things like this, right?'

'We?'

'Yes, we. Teachers. We're always being watched.'

'Don't wear it to school. Wear it outside.'

She laughed. 'What? We have to be even more responsible outside, Miss Ambika. Parents, students, everyone is watching us everywhere.' Her voice dipped 'Even our peers. *Especially* our peers. We're representatives of CVS even in our off time. We need to set the right example.'

'So everyone will have a problem with us looking normal?'

She sighed. 'You're no longer normal, Miss Ambika. You're a teacher.'

I didn't know what she meant. She always took things a bit too seriously than I thought necessary. But then the other day I went for a run and understood exactly what she was talking about. A lady from the neighbourhood stopped me and introduced herself.

'Hello ji! I'm Guggi Chaddha. My daughter's in Grade II. You teach at CVS?'

I really had not wanted to stop but she'd started jogging with me. 'Yes. I'm on my run so …'

'Just wanted to ask,' she persevered as she started jogging with me breathlessly, 'whether term break will happen as per schedule? Because we have to book tickets. To London.'

I looked down at her dainty kitten heels. 'Are those good to run in?'

'No!' she said breathlessly and grabbed my arm to make me stop too. She panted a little as I reluctantly stopped and made a deliberate show of pulling out my AirPods. 'Will they?'

'I have no idea. You should write to the school and find out.'

'But you're a class teacher.'

'Believe it or not, there's only so much that we know!' I waved to her and started to jog again as another lady joined her and looked at my bare legs in disgust.

'She's a teacher at Champion Valley? Look at how she's dressed.'

I pretended not to hear as Guggi Chaddha tried to shush her.

'Standards are really falling.'

I stopped and turned around to face them. 'Sorry?'

'What if some student sees you?' the other woman replied. Guggi Chaddha tried to silence her again.

'Excuse me? So what if they see me?'

She didn't say anything, just looked me up and down. I turned around and continued with my jog.

'You're a teacher. You should dress more decently!' she called out after me.

So I did something I regretted. I held up my middle finger.

Thank god, it didn't circle back to school, but I did tell Dodo, and as expected, he sounded pretty exasperated. And amused.

Lesson Seven
Unit Test

From: Ambika S <Ambika.s@cvs.in>
To: III B Parents Group
Date: 8 August 2022 at 2:41 PM
Sub: Revision Test

Dear Parents,

As discussed during the orientation, Grade III will be having marked tests starting this month. A more detailed note by our grade coordinator, Shilpa, is attached herewith.

Regards,

Ambika S.
Class Teacher, III B

From: Ambika S <Ambika.s@cvs.in>
To: III B Parents Group
Date: 8 August 2022 at 2:43 PM
Sub: Re: Revision Test

Please read that as detailed note by grade coordinator, MISS Shilpa Anand, is attached herewith.

Regards,

Ambika S.
Class Teacher, III B

Riddhi

Weight: 73.4 kgs
Diet Plan: Carb-free

Syra is so happy, so happy, don't even ask. She loves tests. I told her if she loves tests so much she should get blood test and stool test also done.

'I don't like tests because I'm competitive, Ma, I like them because I like a good challenge,' she said like an annoyingly sensible eighty-year-old lady.

Pata nahin, I toh never liked tests. Maybe because I didn't like to cheat. My friend Anita toh used to carry so many farrey—you know, chits—hidden in her socks and her bra and her naada and all that, but I toh said who are you tricking if not yourself? Come to think of it, she used to call me 'Maa Riddhi Devi' because I was always being philosophical, so maybe Syra gets that from me. Anyway, Anita said if she didn't do well she would have to marry Raju halwai, whereas she wanted to marry Pinku halwai. Finally Raju halwai turned his mithai shop into cool café so she dropped Pinku like a hot jalebi. She cheated on her exams and on her lover, so I stopped being friends with her.

Except when I go that side and want discount on coffee, then I call her. So she's more like my friends with benefits.

Anyway, as expected, Rekha Tandon called me right before test season started. She likes to keep a tab on Syra like a mother-in-law only. I hope so, hope so, hope so Syra doesn't grow up and marry her Aseer! So many nightmares I have!

'What's the syllabus for the science test?' Rekha Tandon asked me so sweetly I thought thank god it's carb-free diet day otherwise, I wouldn't have to put jam on my toast only—I'd get diabetes with this.

'Bhai, I toh don't know,' I brushed her off. 'Syra reads emails and portal, and does revision herself only.'

'Oh, yes, of course, yes, yes. Even Aseer.'

Which is big fat lie! I know Rekha Tandon spoon-feeds her son everything for tests. I feel so bad also because he's actually very good cricket player but Rekha Tandon only wants him to come first only like my Syra.

'So then why you wanted to know syllabus from me if you already know?' I asked direct to Rekha Tandon. I don't make mince of my words.

'I just wanted to cross-check. I mean, I'm a working woman, na, so I feel so disconnected.'

Uff! This working woman thing again. Everyone acted like it was such a big deal I wasn't working. And everyone thought I should know everything happening at school too just because I was homestay mother. Sorry, stay-at-home mother.

'Yes, yes, I understand,' I said casually. 'Even my best friend, Jia, na, Rabia's mother, she's also working.' I liked to boast about Jia. But it reminded me, even Jia would not know syllabus. So after making nonsense polite talk with Rekha Tandon, I made Syra send a long message to Auntyji telling her what Rabia had to study for test. Then I forwarded to Jia also. Three days later, she answered my message.

> What's this?

Hai! Beda gark! I called her.
'Test syllabus.'
'What test?'
'Unit tests, na, they're starting.'
'Was there an email?'

Jia was gone case! I told her not to worry, I had told Auntyji already. And then gave her lecture on how to be involved mum. Which was unfair because I knew she was doing her best.

Anyway, when tests began, I realized something about myself.

First, science test: Syra got 20/20, but so did Ahaan Dotwalla. Then the English test happened, Syra got 20/20, but so did Ahaan Dotwalla. Then maths, again both 20/20. Matlab, I'm not competitive or anything, but only when he got 16/20 in Hindi and Syra got 20/20 I got saas mein saas. Means, I breathed sigh of relief. Thank god Syra is only topper!

When I went to pick up Syra—I do car pick up, na; no bus-shus for the kids, Papaji, my FIL, insists—I told Miss Ambika I heard Hindi test was tough. She looked at me blankly, I think so my wearing a tiara was bit much since I was coming back from family kitty, but then she said she didn't believe in tests. I was toh so shocked. Teacher doesn't believe in tests? Then why she is taking tests? Mad woman! Total mad!

Pareeta

Week 25

Tests really bring out the worst in parenting. It's suddenly you taking the test instead of your children. I had also learnt the hard way. With Vidya, I would sit before every test for revisions, make sheets for her, maintain a timetable, ensure she got enough practice, enough food, enough sleep. I would ask her to recall questions when she got home from school with no patience to even wait for the result to come in, fret over things like handwriting and spellings and every mark lost. I knew how much of an impression it made on the teacher—they would categorize the smart ones over the not-so-smart ones and always push the smart ones across platforms. I would spend hours making her projects, treat her homework as my own, get her unlimited tuitions if needed. I was such a helicopter mom.

But with Aryan, as a second-time mother, I'd just handed over the controls to him. He would make his own projects, he would do his homework himself, study for tests himself, he would do everything on his own, have confidence in his success and take responsibility for his own failure.

Unfortunately, that strategy bombed.

I sat with his corrected maths and science sheet. 8/20. 12/20. Vidya walked past us eating a bowl of popcorn.

'Duffer,' she said moving on to collapse on the couch.

'Vidya, don't speak to your brother like that.'

'Why? I never got anything less than 19 or 20 out of 20. He's got an 8!'

Aryan had not an iota of guilt on his face. 'Kevin got 6.'

How did my son think comparing his already low marks with lower marks helped?

'Then you're both duffers,' Vidya announced chewing on the popcorn.

'Vidya, I don't want such language in the house. Aryan, irrespective of anyone else's performance, yours has to be at least on par with the class.' I got a cramp and winced. Aryan noticed it and for the first time stopped smiling.

'You don't have to get so upset, Mom. You look like you're going to cry.'

'I'm fine. I'm fine. I just need a glass of water.' I took a sip and turned back to his paper. 'Air is blue in colour. How is air blue, Aryan? Can you see air right now?'

'The sky is blue and that's all air. Anyway, Miss Ambika said not to worry about the marks. She said as long as we understood the concepts, it's okay.'

'But you've obviously not understood the concepts! That's why the low marks!'

Aryan started kicking the football he was playing with. 'Nutmeg!' he said gleefully, kicking the ball between my legs.

'Aryan, leave the ball and listen to me.'

'I *am* listening! Miss Ambika said just to get the papers signed, but not to worry! She thinks we're all fine and doesn't understand why we have to have marked tests in Grade III anyway.'

I was shocked. 'Miss Ambika said that? To you?'

'To the whole class.'

'This is totally inappropriate!' It was one thing that the teacher was crazy and sent rude emails in the middle of the night, but to disagree with the academic outlook and discipline of the school so openly with the children was quite another. I wanted to send an email immediately.

'Mom,' Vidya called out. 'What's wrong with you? You're quite high-strung.'

'What?'

'I mean, it is only a test. And you're never this agitated by marks.'

'Of course I am! I used to be so particular with yours too.'

Vidya looked at me squarely but didn't say anything. Then she got up and went to her room.

I sat there trying to calm myself down. It was just a test. Just a test. But Aryan's performance was a reflection on my parenting. Because I was raising him single-handedly, it all came down to me.

I took out my phone and typed an email to the teacher marking the grade coordinator.

Giselle

Time: 12.26 a.m.
Unread emails (2,878)

Rajiv and I both stared at the maths test paper.
'To be fair, neither of us was very good at maths,' he said with a dismissive shrug.

'To not be good at and to flunk it are two very different things,' I told him.

'You win some, you lose some.'

'Just the attitude I would want my lawyer to have when he fights my case.'

'You're being too harsh.'

'I'm being practical. I'm writing to the teacher. She's obviously not doing a good enough job of teaching.'

Rajiv sighed. 'How many emails have you sent this month?'

'What?'

'How many emails to the school?'

I got really cross. 'Rajiv Savarkar, if I don't raise issues then nothing will work. The school will start taking parents for granted. Have you not seen how terrible this Ambika teacher is? Look at how badly Kevin's doing!'

'He did get like 52 per cent in science. Maybe he'll be a scientist.'

'Maybe. If he ever graduates from Grade III.'

'You're overreacting.'

FFS! *I* was overreacting. I always knew Kevin wasn't academically inclined, but then that was the point of putting him in CVS. So that he'd get the best of teachers and the best of teaching methodology, and make the best of whatever he has. I had hoped never to engage with external help but with these sort of marks, we had to make some dent in his schedule to fit in maths, Hindi and English tuitions. Maybe science was a mix up too. Maybe he copied from Aryan on that test. Or from that Ahaan kid who seems to be giving Syra Chhabra a run for her money. I wished the school would take more responsibility and not leave us to fend for ourselves like this, looking for teachers outside of the establishment but it had really come to that. I started to type out an email.

'Gis, they're already giving them decent education. Now this is only you reacting to their performance.'

'They're killing the child's self-confidence by marking him.'

'Our child is unperturbed, Gis. It's only you who's reacting.'

'How come you're not reacting? Because you don't feel responsible for his performance ... That's it! You think it's the mother's job.'

'Don't make this a feminist issue, Gis.'

'How else am I supposed to read it? I'm panicked about how he's falling behind his peers while you're chilling like it'll work out magically. Who'll do the magic, Rajiv? Me?'

'I have no such expectations of you. Voodoo, yes. Magic, no.'

Oh, his sense of humour! I ignored him. 'Everyone at school will think, oh that Giselle Savarkar; she's so busy she doesn't spend time on her son's education.'

'Nobody's judging you. How does it even matter what anyone says?'

'It matters to me. And that's that!'

I stomped out of the room only to find Kevin sprawled out on the bed with an encyclopaedia. He looked up at me and snapped the book shut.

'Are you angry with me because of my marks?'

It was the perfect moment for me to drive home the point of how he's always wasting his time. But he looked so concerned, I sat down on the bed. 'No, I don't think your teacher's doing a good enough job of teaching.'

'Miss Ambika? But she's great.'

'In what way?'

'Aryan says she's chill.'

'What does that mean?'

'It means we can ask her anything in class and we can talk out of turn, and Miss Shilpa hates it … And she's always getting into trouble because we make so much noise, but Miss Ambika herself is very chill.'

So there was no discipline in the classroom. She was trying to gain popularity rather than teach the students.

Who was she exactly and how had she managed to get into CVS? I had to send that email.

Ambika

Holy fuck!

If I thought I got too many emails from parents every day, the number had exploded exponentially during test time. It must've been simpler back when emails didn't exist. Who would spend time writing letters? But now, it's at the click of a button you've got your point across. And boy, was it a lot of points across!

As it is, I was exhausted from grading all those papers—an unnecessary bullshit system to evaluate the comprehension levels of the students and I had said so to Shilpa Anand herself, but she had instead sat me down and lectured me at the benefits of taking tests.

'It'll build their self-confidence, develop self-reliance, learn to accept success and failure, provide them the fullness of learning, and prepare them for life. It's not a test, Miss Ambika. It's not marks. It's a life skill. You must make sure they learn to handle stress at a younger age, so that it becomes a most natural part of their lives. When does life not test us, Miss Ambika? We may not be graded but every day we face tests in many ways. Then Jake met Mindy and Polly got jealous and committed felony but the detective was …' Obviously she didn't say the last bit. It's just my mind having wandered off because she sounded batshit crazy.

When she had made enough of her impassioned speech, I'd asked her whether I was free to communicate with parents the way I wanted in response to their various brilliant queries, but Shilpa Anand was adamant we use the 'manual' from the 'Testing at CVS' training. She promptly emailed me a 108-slide presentation on the same. If CVS was known for its systems, Shilpa Anand was its worthy mascot. I would never open that document.

I thanked her profusely for her time and turned back to my emails which looked like a scene out of *The Matrix*, the way they were rolling in. I couldn't be bothered reading them anymore. In any case, the children were back from their recess for the much-hated maths class. They had no idea how lucky they had it with me. I was dying to tell them my own maths teacher was now the principal of the school. Would they prefer her instead?

Anyway, we were learning the concept of division today. I had no idea why we were to start a topic right before the end of the term, but here we were, thirty blank faces and one knowing one trying to grasp the topic. I wasn't the knowing one, by the way. That was Syra. I was just trying to repeat the lesson plan verbatim.

'Okay, let me try explaining again.'

So I did. Again. And again. And again. Some of them actually got it. Some of them still did not. As per the plan, I had to give them three written problems today and we had ten minutes left in class, having gotten pretty much nowhere.

'Miss Ambika,' Ahaan moaned, 'you always tell us to be honest with you, so I'm doing that. Division is so hard.'

'It's not!' Syra argued.

'Yeah,' Prabh agreed. 'You just think it's hard, so it's hard!'

There were arguments on both sides and I was exhausted already, but what Prabh said struck a chord.

'Okay, let's do an activity,' I said, knowing fully well what I was going to do would be disruptive and Shilpa Anand would come racing down the corridor to stop us, but so be it. 'Kids, stand up and do forty jumping jacks.'

They all stood up grudgingly, dragging their chairs and their tables, some moaning, some giggling—however, I knew they were certainly more invested now than they were during my earlier one-way monologue.

'Begin.'

They started together, then some started speeding ahead, one of them started laughing hysterically, one banged into the table, so more laughter, some of the more competitive ones started counting faster to finish first, someone's shorts kept slipping off, a couple of them got impatient and cheated, but, by the end of it, they were all breathless but more awake.

'Okay, well done. Tired?'

As expected, some were honest and some were defiant.

'Let's do it again. Only this time we do ten jumping jacks and take a two-minute break, then another ten. We will do this four times. Start.'

So the whole exercise started again, then we took a break and started again, and repeated two more times. Then I made them sit down.

'Now, did you find doing it the second time around easier? Just ten jumping jacks instead of forty together?'

Some of them disagreed, but I decided to go with the answer I wanted to hear, which was yes, it was easier to do four sets of ten.

'See? Dividing something into smaller parts makes things easier. Therefore, it's important to learn division and now that you know dividing is helpful, you'll find the concept of division easier too!'

I knew I was using psychology on a group of unsuspecting eight-year-olds, but there was a chance it would work. I started explaining the concept again. This time, everyone was a bit more engaged.

As expected, Shilpa Anand had noticed the chaos in the classroom and was standing near a window with a frown upon her brow. I decided to ignore her. Then I wrote down the three questions we had to do on the blackboard and asked them to solve it in their notebooks.

After the bell rang and the class left for music, I sat down at my desk and saw Shilpa Anand walking in, a mix of curiosity and annoyance on her face.

'What was that all about?' she asked.

I gave her a nonchalant shrug. 'Oh, that was nothing. Just wanted to wake them up.'

'By making them do PE?'

'Yeah, you have to mix it up sometimes,' I said making a pile of their submitted maths notebooks.

'But they understood the concept of division through it?'

I shrugged again. 'Well, they enjoyed it more, certainly.'

She looked at me strangely, picking up a notebook and flipping through it. I prayed it was Syra's, but it was Kevin's and, oh gosh, his was a bit of a nightmare. I quickly busied myself with my emails. Shilpa Anand studied his notebook for a minute, flipped through a couple of chapters and then snapped it shut.

'Interesting, Miss Ambika. Very interesting,' she said mysteriously and walked away.

I waited for her to leave before grabbing Kevin's notebook and racing to the division page. All three sums were correct. I breathed a sigh of relief. Then I turned to my open screen of incoming emails.

> Can you give us an extra class on ...
>
> Can you spend more time on ...
>
> Can you explain this concept to ...
>
> Can you suggest a home tutor for ...

I put in an auto-response and sent it to all the emails.

> Let's discuss it at the upcoming PTM.

Lesson Eight
Recess

From: Ambika S <Ambika.s@cvs.in>
To: III B Parents Group
Date: 15 September 2022 at 7:48 AM
Sub: PTM

Dear Parents,

The term is coming to a close.

To discuss your child's academic and social progress, kindly attend the scheduled Parent-Teacher Meeting on 30 September 2022 as per the attached slots.

Please note: Requests for exchange of slots will not be entertained. Please be punctual.

Regards,

Ambika S.
Class Teacher, III B

Ambika

I once dated a guy who worked in sales. He was this wonderful, cheerful person, who turned into some sort of stressed-out monster every end of month. He wouldn't eat, he wouldn't sleep, he would be on calls, on his laptop and sweated profusely, literally and figuratively. We broke up in three months because I never understood that sort of stress.

Now, PTMs are to teachers what month ends are to sales guys. I have never been as stressed as I have been this week. Not only were we gunning to complete our curriculum, we were putting to test all our skills at creative writing. CVS had a policy of providing a personal touch. Which meant every report card was handwritten, had two pictures of the student in their academic and non-academic environment, and quotes from what they said in class. I wanted to tear my hair out.

'You need to give constructive feedback,' Shilpa Anand had told us in our last training session on report-card writing. I nodded off at least thrice and Sahiba had to nudge me awake. The acceptable etiquette on report-card writing was never ending. You are no longer even allowed to say 'needs improvement'—you have to say 'needs practice'. You can't say 'can't do maths'—you have to say 'leaning towards creativity'. You can't say 'rude and undisciplined'—you have to say 'of an independent mindset'. You can't say 'doesn't pay attention'—you have to say 'shows inclination towards free-thinking'. I'm all for it, of course. But, at the end of the day, a report card does end up being judgemental on your child's capabilities. Syra was a genius, Nolan was an idiot and everyone else was just the same—equally sweet and annoying. More annoying than sweet, if I was being honest. I had to employ a lot of story-weaving to get through some of the report cards and had a thesaurus open at all times. How many ways can you say the same thing?

Shilpa Anand came to me looking very worried as I sat with my fists in my hair one Saturday, trying to think of how to say 'her grammar sucks' creatively.

'Do you need some help, Miss Ambika? Perhaps you could go back to my presentation on how to write impactful report cards?'

Or maybe I could smack my head on a boulder?

'I'm just taking a break,' I said politely.

'Well, today is Saturday and we will need to sign them by Monday.'

'I know. I'm working on it.'

She looked at me doubtfully, then pulled up a chair. 'We at CVS believe ...' Fuckkkkk! Another sermon was on its way. I quickly averted my eyes to my mail. As expected, as soon as my email with the PTM timings had gone out, responses had started pouring in for a change in time slots. Sometimes the same couple asked for different slots. They could at least coordinate things between themselves!

It was so annoying. They were so annoying. What would be really cool would be to give an honest report card on the parents instead of the children! Tell them off for the shitheads that they are. I was so done with them!

'Why don't you take notes?' Shilpa Anand's voice interrupted me.

'Sorry?'

'Notes on what I'm saying. It'll be really helpful.'

'Uh ... Of course.'

I pulled out a sheet of paper and pretended to write.

'Number one,' she said pacing the room, 'dressing for the PTM. You must wear clothes that do not make them feel intimidated. We're trying to create a safe environment here. We're trying to tell them their children spend the entire day with responsible, decent adults who take our position seriously. How we dress really communicates that; dress like them!'

Ha! Then I'd probably spend my day switching outfits. I'd wear a ballroom gown for Syra's mum, a business suit for Giselle Savarkar, a saree for the politician one, a little black number for the dad who spoke to my chest a lot.

'Always keep a helpful, hospitable face.'

Like I'm a receptionist at a hotel. Or an airline attendant. Tea or coffee? Maths or English?

'They must open up to you. They must feel like you love their child like yours.'

My issue was that they were opening up a bit too much to me. I felt like I knew all about their private lives. All their little secrets came tumbling out once their miniature versions walked into the class.

'Miss Ambika, something was up in my parents' room last night.'

'Really?'

'Yes. Mummy sounded very upset.'

'Like a fight? Sometimes we need to give them privacy and not worry too much about it because—'

'Not a fight. She was making lots of strange noises.'

'Oh! Ohhhh! ... Now, Shaan, what you heard was—'

'The Conjuring. I know. They were watching The Conjuring. It scares my mother a lot. They watch Netflix once we're asleep.'

If only the parents knew how much I knew about them.

I realized Shilpa Anand was going on and on, not paying any attention to me. So I bit back a smile and did what my heart told me to do. Something more exciting than writing report cards on kids. I started writing a report card on the parents. More specifically, on the fabulous mums of Champion Valley!

I started with my favourite.

Dear Giselle Savarkar,

Congratulations on your diploma in complaint-writing! You are outstanding! Unfortunately, your people skills are significantly below standards. From the canteen to the classroom, we seem to be doing nothing right. And you are so kind to hold up a mirror to us. Here's a reflection of you. Constantly raising issues does not make you a better parent. Shouting louder than someone else does not make you right. You're fooling no one by pretending to be involved. Also, who are you trying to fool with those contact lenses?

Dear Syra's Mum, Riddhi Makheeja Chhabra (RMC!),
You are a fashion stylist's dream come true! Or a nightmare, however you choose to think of it. One never knows whether you'll come dressed as a princess out of a fairytale or a bride at a Punjabi wedding. Your network is stronger than Vodafone's. Is there anyone you don't know the insider dope on? You are a social butterfly that literally looks like a butterfly! Your daughter is a delight—mature, smart, curious and kind. But you're almost embarrassed by her excellence. It's always your son you speak of but not of your genius girl. Is there a bit of misogyny you're trying to conceal?

Dear Rabia's Mum,
Another one who leads a fabulous life! Hotshot at some corporate or something, and drenched in make-up. It's blinding! It's really cool to have an American accent but it's also telling of being a wannabe. Also there's zero response to my messages. Zero. For someone who works in IT, do you even know how emails work?

Dear Pregnant Pareeta,
How are you even having this baby? Your son hasn't seen his father in years, he claims. You already have two perfect children. Plus Kevin! So why this one? To save your marriage?

And, of course ...

> *Dear Celebrity Wife Kainaz,*
> *What is with the reverse snobbery? Why do you look almost disdainful of everything? You're in Delhi; let go off Goa. Your innocent little boy reports back every grudge you hold against the city. You're letting your negativity rub off on him!*

> *Dear Rekha Tandon,*
> *Your sindoor ...*

'Got it?'

I jumped in my seat as I saw Shilpa Anand watching me. I quickly covered my notes and nodded.

'Great. I hope the PTM will be fruitful, and you'll view report-card writing as a joyful exercise and not a boring task.'

Oh, there was certainly nothing boring about it now!

Giselle

Time: 8.02 p.m.
Unread emails (3,008)

Nobody was willing to work for the goddamn toilet client. Silky, 'I'm from IIM', had named it Project Flush, but after reaching out to sixteen worthy candidates and failing, I couldn't see any humour in it. There was a 12 per cent commission on this and I wasn't willing to let it go.

'We could rename it Project Constipation,' she'd sighed. I was in no mood for more toilet humour.

So I was once again scanning CV after CV on a Friday morning before the dreaded PTM, while Rajiv sang in the shower. When he emerged, I was speaking to someone in Finland, dangling a carrot for him to come back.

'The money's good, Gis, but I don't think rural India is my scene,' the candidate said.

I gnashed my teeth. 'Gis'! As if we were childhood buddies. And since when was rural India not his scene? He'd risen from a small town—if it could be called a town or even qualified for 'small'—but now he acted like he was the king of the world. I tried not to get personal. I was a thorough professional after all. I'd called him because not only was he right for the job, the job was right for him. I decided to remind him of a few things.

'Ramesh, here's the thing. The last time we spoke, you were keen to come back to India because of your parents and your wife. Kamla, isn't it?' I read from my notes.

'That's right.'

'So you'd said Kamla wanted to get back to her job here and you weren't saving enough there, your parents were ageing, you needed to return to the country and you quoted a pay range which this one meets.'

'Yes, but—'

'I would have waited to get you another opportunity, but you're someone who's grounded in India, you've done stints in rural India, you've grown brands, you've seen distribution channels, you're insightful, you're rooted.'

'But, Gis ... It's toilets!'

'They're hygiene products and the sector has huge government backing. This will give you the career stability you want. This will not only enhance your expertise but also make you invaluable to the industry. You can be the data bank while making a social difference—everything you had said you'd wanted when we had connected four years ago.'

'You have a great memory.'

Flattery would get him nowhere. 'I want you to think about what I'm saying, Ramesh.' I continued with more of my notes and arguments, and the one pager Silky had prepared on why this candidate would be suitable.

He finally sighed. 'Okay, Gis. I'll get back to you.'

'Take your time but let me know by tomorrow morning, India time. And the name's Giselle.'

When I hung up, I saw Rajiv watching me. 'What?' I asked typing in an update on the system so that someone else could call candidates when I was in school.

'You're pretty awesome,' Rajiv said in a strange voice. I looked up at him and realized that the strangeness was affection. FFS!

'Let's go. We're late,' I told him sternly. I had no time for romance so early in the morning.

'Wasn't the PTM at 10?'

'I swapped it with Pareeta. We're going in at 8.'

'I thought the class teacher said we can't change slots?'

'And why is her word gospel?'

I switched off my screen and stood up to leave.

'Gis, aren't you forgetting something?'

I looked at him and he raised his eyebrows. I turned to catch my reflection in the mirror. Oh!

Kainaz

	The teacher interaction. Top 5 points:
1.	She wore a saree that she looked positively uncomfortable in. Why had she bothered with it? I'd come to think CVS didn't believe in being all that traditional. But today she looked like she had draped on a hot air balloon. She really should have pinned it up.
2.	She had nothing to really say. She kept saying, oh he's fine. He's doing fine. Even when we flipped through his notebooks, everything was marked in red but also had 'good job' scribbled. I thought his spellings were atrocious and was shocked she'd given him 20/20 in so many tests, but she said his concepts are clear and that's all that matters. I don't understand the school at all.
3.	I asked her if he had settled in, had friends. She said it was super easy to make friends at this age and that I shouldn't worry.
4.	Then towards the end of all the hmm-hawws, finally her eyes lit up, and she said Ahaan does beautiful art and we should make sure we *never* train him professionally. What was she talking about? Yes, Ahaan was forever drawing but his drawings were squiggles—not *art* art! Maybe she was so lost, she got Ahaan confused. So I enunciated politely and told her I was talking about

	Ahaan from Goa! To which she smiled a really small smile and told me, yes, but he was now Ahaan from Gurgaon. It was almost passive-aggressive.
5.	And lastly, Varaz. I looked over at him many times during the PTM but he was just staring at her. I had never seen him stare at a woman like this before, almost gaping. It must have made her uncomfortable because she refused to meet his eye and had the entire conversation with me. Before we went to bed I finally asked him why he had been looking at Miss Ambika that way. He said she looked familiar and was trying to place her. I'd thought so too honestly. She looked like a model. He agreed.

Riddhi

Weight: 74.1 kgs
Diet Plan: Gulab jamun to celebrate Syra's report card. Cake to celebrate Shivam's. Rasmalai to celebrate Harsh's sale of Westend farmhouse. Ice cream to celebrate five years of Glam Girls kitty. Mathura ka peda to celebrate Mummy's return from Mathura. Rasgulla to celebrate midnight.

Syra insists on coming for report card day. It's good only. I don't know what to talk to teacher about.

It feels like two different universes for both of them. Shivam teacher was just complaining, complaining and I told her, madam, it's okay if he brings toys to school sometimes, you can use it in show and tell. But teacher says she doesn't know what show and tell to do with Hulk or Iron Man. I suggested, most kindly, that you make children learn H for Hulk, I for Iron Man because that's how I teach Shivam at home. He also says K for kick and P for punch, but I didn't tell her that. Besides, I don't teach Shivam anything. He has a tuition master coming in. I think the only reason he comes is because we serve pakodas with chai but he comes twice a week even though Syra says it's a very bad habit.

'Let him learn in school, Mama. He won't pay attention otherwise.'

'Everyone's not like you, Gudiya. Shivam needs help.'

'He needs discipline.'

See? Eight going on eighty.

Anyway, teacher kept saying, 'Cannot believe he's Syra's brother,' and I was like why? They have exact same nose and mouth. In fact, if you see my childhood photos, ditto me. Syra rolled her eyes and asked the teachers if there are any improvement areas for Shivam, and I wanted to tell her, well there's one for you. Manners! When I'm there, why you have to interfere? But teacher presented list anyway.

Then we went to Miss Ambika, and she toh saw me and dropped the whole bundle of report cards she was carrying. Then spent next five minutes trying to pick up only. I toh couldn't help since I was wearing stitched on golden saree—they have pockets now na—but Harsh could, and he was wearing his one-size-too-small, hot-green, metallic three-piece suit. Maybe that's what had surprised her and she'd dropped the papers.

As I sat and looked around, I realized, very untidy classroom she has. It looked like Shivam's bedroom only. Maybe I could send Lalita Didi once to help clear up. Matlab so much print outs, so much paper, so much scribbles. Uff! It looked like sarkari office. Harsh also said it looked like Mini Secretariat where you go for registry.

Then, when she gave us report card, I died of heart attack! I was like hain! Needs practice, needs practice! I said Miss Ambika, but Syra is topper. Now what practice? Should she become doctor?

Then she looked totally shocked and realized report cards were mixed up. She said sorry, sorry, excuse me for ten minutes and asked us to wait outside till she sorted it out. Next door class teacher, Miss Sahiba, also came to help her with the papers as did Miss Shilpa Anand. I gave Miss Sahiba a big air kiss because she used to be Syra's KG teacher.

By god, that wait was the best part of PTM day. Outside so many people I met. Amruta–Amrita duo coming to discuss their daughters, Kiera and Kaira, and then Rekha Tandon, commented on my saree but I toh didn't compliment back on her black tracksuit. 'Juicy' written on her big bottom, I thought is just too much.

Everyone then started saying 'wah-wah' that Syra has been topping again and I was like that's old news. Then we gossiped some more. Finally, a very, what's the right word—fluttered?—flustered-looking Miss Ambika came out and called us in as the other two teachers apologized for the mix up and left.

I sat down on the chair and looked at her. She looked totally nervous. 'So, Miss Ambika, what's new?' I asked politely.

Lesson Nine
Drama

Dodo

> DODO!

> Answer the phone!

> DODO!!!!!

> You'd better be dead Dodo if you're not answering my phone

> I've called you six times!

> Ok I'm now worried. Calling your mom

> > Hey. Just saw. Was in security check. Getting onto a flight. Will call

> No! No will call!

> Answer!

> Now your phone is off. Fuck!

> Get ready for the longest text of your life because this is urgent and I need you to see it the minute you land

> Remember how I was joking that I should write a report card on the parents instead of the students and you told me I'm crazy?

> Well, I did it anyway

> I know! Shit!

> It gets worse

> I don't know where the paper's gone

> I've spent all day looking for it!!!!!!

> I only know it was lying in a pile near the signed report cards but I can't find it. So shit shit shit shit shit!

> Shit shit shit shit shit shit shit!

> Shit shit shit shit shit!

> Call me as soon as you land

> PS: Mrs Mehta's going to kill me!

Pareeta

Week 32

I thought I'd get the mums together during the term break. Not all the mums. Just Riddhi, Jia, Kainaz and Giselle. The normal moms. Giselle laughed when I named the group that because she said every single moms' group that gets formed is called 'Normal Moms' since they think everyone else is abnormal. But it was true. I thought at least these moms were different. They didn't sprout designer bags or go on ultra- fancy vacations and generally had more substance than the others.

As expected, Riddhi texted me on the side asking me why I thought Giselle was normal. Nothing about her snooty personality and condescending attitude felt normal to her. But I told her Giselle was my friend and was really nice once you get to know her. Also, as expected, Giselle declined the plan saying she had to be at work even on a Saturday. Jia also said she'd drop in after two as she had meetings, but Riddhi coerced her into leaving early and offered to pick her up herself.

They arrived dot on time. Riddhi instructed her driver to bring in a basket of fruit and I gasped at the size of it.

'Riddhi! This can feed the entire colony!'

'I thought you bake so much, it will be helpful for you to bake something healthy for a change, na!'

I didn't know whether to be offended or touched as I did a lot of healthy baking already but, before I could offer some to her, she reached out for the cheese-loaded toast I had just taken out of the oven and put it in her mouth, whole.

'Yum! Bohot badhiya!'

'Where are the kids?' I asked them as they settled down.

'Syra and Shivam have gone to Nanu–Nani house,' Riddhi said. 'My nanny is on leave, na. So no nanny means job for Nani. Also, only FIL is there at my place. And yesterday my FIL's BP went so high, so high, I couldn't leave Shivam around him. He's so irresponsible. My FIL, not Shivam. He had three Amritsari kulchas with butter and masala pyaaz. Do you know how much salt there is in masala pyaaz? I said also, Papaji, just have kulcha with butter, but he wanted his onion. Had to have high BP!'

'Er ... I hope he's okay?'

'Oh, he's very happy! My mother has bought him two-two new NERF guns.'

I blinked at her wondering why Riddhi's mother has brought her father-in-law NERF guns but she clarified it was for Shivam.

'And where's Rabia?' I asked politely.

'She's home,' Jia said. 'Some online Zoom party for her friend back home.' I realized she still referred to the US as 'home'.

'How did Aryan do on maths test?' Riddhi asked reaching out for a bruschetta. 'Syra said he got 10/20?'

'Yes, maths isn't his strong point.'

'She said Kevin also got 10? Giselle Savarkar must have complained.'

'Isn't Giselle your neighbour?' Jia asked as the Didi brought out lemonade.

'She stays one floor above us,' I told Jia.

The bell rang and I guessed it was Kainaz. She stood there uncertainly, holding a little present.

'I got this for you.'

Riddhi's eyes lit up as she saw her and she quickly swallowed her third bruschetta. 'Today toh you must give us Bollywood gossip, Kainazji. Pareetaji, are these made of atta?'

'I'm afraid not,' I apologized. 'But I could make you a salad if you want to eat healthy?'

'Never! Today my diet is tomato only again. Every few days, he gives me tomato diet. I feel like Santa Claus!'

'Can there be a diet like that?' Jia asked doubtfully.

'Yes, this is fine though. Bruschetta has raw tomatoes.'

'I wish you'd told me. I would've made something more appropriate,' I offered.

'No worries. I'll just put some sauce on the food, so it'll be tomato. Anyway, Kainazji, start!'

But just then the bell rang. Riddhi immediately left her plate and patted her mouth, as if expecting Varaz Dotwalla. But surprisingly, in walked Giselle.

'I had an hour before the meeting, so I thought I'd join in. What are we having? Red or white?'

Kainaz

	How an actually divergent group of mums is similar (a revelation!):
1.	Juggling: We were all juggling. Responsibilities, roles, multitasking. We already knew that. There were so many articles on it, the internet spoke about it. It felt good to be acknowledged. Yet, one stray comment that we have it 'easy' irked us, made us doubt ourselves, our purpose, our contribution to the family—especially towards the children.
2.	Our children: We loved talking about our children. And, for once, around other mothers, we could talk about them and obsess over them as much as we liked without being judged. They were such a huge part of our identity. Even someone as strong and successful as Giselle Savarkar was unapologetically anchored to her son.
3.	Competitive: There was always a subtle competition about the children, even though the definition was conveniently altered. We wanted them to sound like specimen, laughing at one's plight, whilst also thinking, thank god your child isn't a brat. Or the relief that it's not only your child who acts so ... child-like.

4.	Maids: We loved talking about our maids. This was pretty unique to Delhi. Toddy Amma had stayed with us for generations back in Goa. I'd had six changes in six months in Delhi.
5.	Labour: Mothers loved to bond over labour stories. Throw in a group of strangers and it takes them five minutes to discuss their gory labour. There's always a competition on who had it worse. Or more comical. Your water broke? Ten points. Your husband panicked? Twenty. Flipping through *What to Expect When You're Expecting* in the labour room? Fifty. Labour upwards of eight years? Hundred. No epidural? Five hundred.
6.	The school: There was nothing that united mums more than a common enemy. And our common enemy today, so fresh after the PTM, was the school. We had the longest discussion on everything that was wrong with the school and the class teacher.
7.	Alcohol: We liked wine. We were on bottle three by now. Nobody kept count of how many reds or whites we were having. Giselle even postponed her meeting.

Riddhi let out a huge, dramatic sigh. 'I didn't know only about homework. Syra toh checks the portal herself and finishes off. Maybe in class only. I can never shout at her for not doing homework. Bloody nuisance!'

'We didn't get any homework in our school in Goa,' I contributed. 'In fact, Ahaan doesn't understand the concept of coming home and doing anything related to school.'

Giselle continued to type on her screen throughout the conversation but seemingly stayed engaged with us too. 'I don't know much about it, but Kev says it's a lot, so I've already complained to their class teacher ... That Miss Ambika.'

'Why do they experiment on our kids only?' Riddhi asked grumpily. 'Giving us brand new, untrained teacher. She looks too much young.'

'I believe she's only thirty,' Pareeta said topping up my glass.

'I've complained to the junior school headmistress,' Giselle said, eyes still on the phone. 'Is she even educationally qualified?'

'But also, where is the time for homework?' Jia continued to argue. 'The bus only comes in at three-thirty.'

'Ours comes in at two,' Pareeta said. 'But Aryan does football with Kevin and—'

'They say two, but it's two-fifteen as per the nanny,' Giselle said looking up angrily from her phone and taking a sip of her wine. 'I've complained to the admin head that there's a problem with the bus timings. Who is the bus vendor, anyway? I plan to email them directly.'

'They're so hungry by the time they reach!' Riddhi complained. 'Syra toh gets back, and makes herself an omelette and butter toast *and* wants smoothie. Now, tell me, which eight-year-old has smoothie? My Shivam toh has full bottle of Bournvita in one go. Sometimes with milk also.'

'Rabia eats nothing,' Jia said.

'I've complained to the canteen manager,' Giselle said. 'They need to be given more satiating meals.'

I guessed no matter what we raised, Giselle had already made a note of it and complained to the authorities. She was perfect for the PTA but wouldn't dare to venture close to it.

We sat down at the dining table, reasonably more relaxed than when we had first started out this afternoon, and I realized, maybe in my headiness, that I liked them. That's right. I think we were on the brink of a friendship.

I had just served myself some of the potato salad when Pareeta's daughter, Vidya, came to the table holding a piece of paper.

'Hey, Mom, you need to see this.'

Ambika

I was jittery. The teachers looked at me like I'd gone crazy because I probably hadn't combed my hair or something and Sahiba, the kindergarten-promoted teacher, even placed a gentle hand on my shoulder and asked me if I was feeling well. I just nodded but didn't speak because I realized I had even forgotten to brush my teeth! After rummaging through my backpack, I found a box of mints that I emptied into the cave of my mouth and told myself to calm down. I must have thrown the paper in the bin or something.

I tried to concentrate on teaching but I was so distracted. Syra had to even remind me to take the attendance. Then, when the bell rang for the prayer assembly, I led them to the playground instead of the hall. All twenty-odd kids stood there, looking at me quizzically. I made some joke about how I was testing whether they were paying attention or not, and then we all sprinted to the assembly hall. Of course, Mrs Mehta pulled us up for running in the corridors and Shilpa Anand looked like she would die of embarrassment on account of me.

Back in class, Rohan forgot to carry his pencil box, so I distractedly handed him my pen. He stood there staring at it like it was a nuclear weapon. That's when I realized we used pencils in class, not pens. Then Youhan did all his work upside down in his notebook by mistake and spent twenty minutes bawling that his mother would get upset. I pacified him telling him it wasn't the end of the world, but it seemed he was more afraid of his mother than of his teacher. How warped was that! Then Kaira or Kiera ripped her shorts and then ripped the other Kaira/Kiera's to ensure she wasn't the only odd one out and a full-on fight broke out. Miss Shilpa walked past just then and shook her head in dismay.

We moved on to our English assignment: Write sentences using the word 'elated'.

I wished him a happy elated buthday.
I was elated to find a colourful unicorn at my doorstep.
I was elated when I went on the eskilator.
I am elated to my mom.

Even that didn't make me laugh.

Finally, I gave them some complicated sums to solve and sat dejected at my desk, pretending to have a headache. I wasn't really pretending since my head was indeed exploding but I thought I'd sold my little act till I saw Syra walk up to my desk.

'Not now, Syra.'

'What's bothering you?' she asked wisely.

I looked up at her, debating how much to tell her. 'I've lost a very important piece of paper.'

'Hmm. Did you mean what you wrote on it?'

Immediately, an alarm bell went off in my head. 'What do you mean?'

'Nothing. Just that the paper you're looking for … It turned up in Aryan's report card.'

Fuck! My heart sank to my knees and my mouth went dry. All the blood rushed to my head and I thought I'd faint.

Syra leaned in. 'I don't know what it said but I heard you said a lot of terrible things about the mums.'

I didn't know what to do so I just stared at her. She placed a hand on mine and looked me squarely in the eye. 'I don't know how much you've messed up this time'—*this* time?—'but we really like you, Miss Ambika. Do something to set it right.'

My heart banged in my chest as she walked back to her seat. Dodo had told me the same thing. Set it right. Do something. Talk to someone. Confess.

The bell rang and I jumped in my seat. The class had erupted in chatter and had started packing their bags. The day had ended. Bus lines were to be formed. Parents would be allowed in through the gate. That's when I noticed Shilpa Anand standing at the door. I pretended to be busy but she didn't budge. I made some mindless small talk with the kids, some of them wondering what had gotten into me suddenly after I'd sulked the whole day, and bid goodbye to all of them very lovingly. Riddhi turned up in a parrot-green outfit and I didn't even bat an eyelid. Finally, Shilpa Anand walked up to me.

'Is there an issue with the class, Miss Ambika?'

I swallowed but tried to appear cool by going through my paperwork. 'Wh ... why?' I stuttered.

'There's an email requesting an urgent meeting with Mrs Mehta from five of your class moms.'

My head started to spin but I shrugged. 'I don't know. I haven't got anything.'

'Well, I've asked her assistant to let them know she's on leave this coming week, but I thought I'd check if something happened.'

I shook my head as she looked at me strangely. I was so tempted to ask which five moms but kept looking at my papers.

'Just thought I'd let you know,' she said and walked away.

I sank into my chair, feeling both numb and flustered. My toes were tingling, my head was throbbing and I had a sudden urge to throw up.

I *had* to do something. I needed someone on my side.

A teacher? No, what would they even say. Maybe they would understand why I did it? Sahiba, maybe? Shilpa Anand herself? Maybe she had a PowerPoint on how to manage screw ups 101?

Or maybe a parent? Someone who could get me an in with the offended mums? Tell them how sorry I was? How it was all untrue? How they were all just indeed fabulous?

'Shilpa!' I called out. I bit my lip. 'Sorry, *Miss* Shilpa. Who were the five mums? I can reach out to them directly?'

'Don't bother. I've told Mrs Mehta's assistant to give them time once she is back.'

'But still. Maybe I'll be able to tell you what happened.'

Shilpa Anand looked at her phone with a frown and scrolled down. 'Kainaz Dotwalla, Giselle Savarkar, Jia Mazumdar, Pareeta Singh, Riddhi Makheeja Chhabra.'

Shit! This was no coincidence. 'Okay. No reason I can think of!' My squeak was so high-pitched, I saw her wince. 'Thanks. Have a good weekend!'

'Today's Monday, Miss Ambika!'

Oh god, whatever! I shrugged, and she shook her head and walked away. I buried my face in my hands. Set it right. Apologize. Where would I start? Which parent? The only one I liked was Pareeta Singh. She was always smiling and was so sweet. Yet, I'd ripped her apart in my note. Why was her pregnancy my business?

I needed someone else.

Giselle Savarkar? Ha ha ha! She must have trained a sniper on me already.

Jia Mazumdar? No thanks. God knows how vengeful she could be with those killer cold eyes of hers.

Riddhi Makheeja Chhabra? Argh!

Kainaz? Wait! Varaz! Varaz Dotwalla! I needed Varaz Dotwalla.

In any case, he owed me.

Lesson Ten
History

From: Ambika S <Ambika.s@cvs.in>
To: III B Parents Group
Date: 1 October 2022 at 10:02 AM
Sub: Dusshera Holidays & Term Break

Dear Parents,

As we take a short break to plan, absorb and implement changes in our academic calendar, please do spend time to strengthen your family bond and re-energize for the coming term.

We also request you to spend some time reflecting on the time gone by and help us define your child's ambitions for the coming term. Kindly fill in the questionnaire (link given below) on the goals you'd like to set for your child so that we can achieve them together.

Happy Dusshera!

Regards,
Ambika S.
Class Teacher, III B

From: Ambika S <Ambika.s@cvs.in>
To: III B Parents Group
Date: 1 October 2022 at 10:05 AM
Sub: Re: Dusshera Holidays

Sorry, link for the goals given below:
https://cvs.in/term2/IIIB/goals

Regards,
Ambika S.
Class Teacher, III B

Jia

'Hotshot at some corporate or something, drenched in make-up. It's blinding!'

It was late in the evening, rain pouring down outside, a chill in the air so characteristic of Bengaluru weather and all the hostel residents were assembled in the mess. Across the long, wooden table was a line-up of pints of beer and I stood looking at my opponent, a shiver of excitement running down my spine. It was the end of 'fresher's week'—seven days of challenges, activities, ice-breakers and parties for all of us newly joined first-year students—and today marked the final event. When the whistle blew, I started glugging down pint after pint, right to the last drop. One bottle, two bottles, three bottles, four … With a huge crowd cheering around me. When the whistle blew to stop, the crowd went berserk, and I wiped the froth off my mouth and grinned. He stood opposite me, still holding his half-finished third pint, defeated yet amused, impressed and watchful. Him, with his droopy eyes, floppy hair and lopsided smile. He raised his bottle to my success and I reached for a fifth one to clink with his. And then the whole college hooted as we held each other's gaze, interlocked our arms and downed our drinks to start our story.

Sahil Saraogi had this air around him—he was charmingly detached, cool, quiet, mysterious and confident. He was so tall that he had a bit of a hunch, so lean, all his clothes were ill-fittingly stylish, his hair was long and floppy, and his eyes always held a hint of bored amusement. He was cryptic and enigmatic, and every girl in college wanted a piece of him. It was also a huge bonus that he came from an affluent business family in Kolkata, but what drew me the most to him was that he was one of the smartest people in class. He coded like it was his first language. He understood machines better than emotions. He could do data, design and analytics with equal ease.

I, on the other hand, had a fire in me. I was a small-town girl, ambitious, competitive, hard-working and bursting to break free from my modest, traditional, restrictive, almost suffocating family roots. I'd jumped at every opportunity to gain exposure outside of Meerut, representing my school at debates, participating in competitive sports, acted onstage, head girl at school, college topper and then aced the entrance exam for a Master's degree in software engineering in a coveted Bangalore college.

I had packed my bags and made a dash for it, promising never to look back, and had been starry-eyed when I'd met the potpourri of people in my college—the privileged, the nerds, the hard-working, the studs. I hadn't known how to slot Sahil Saraogi, other than the fact he looked too relaxed to have too much riding on this course; unlike me, who knew this was my ticket to a better life, to freedom.

So different were Sahil Saraogi and I that we were attracted like two poles of a magnet yet we swirled in a whirlpool of romance over the next two years, oblivious to the world outside, oblivious to our differences.

He smoked up and quoted Marx with as much ease as he broke into old Bollywood numbers at the local dhaba. He fought to reduce the college fees for those who struggled to pay the amount and spent furious amounts of money at expensive restaurants on date nights. He fixed a broken bike chain with the same ease as he launched an e-commerce website. But he'd also discard a shirt when the button broke, or refuse biscuits from a packet that had been lying open too long or flew back home just for a weekend—things I would never dream of doing. He surprised me every day with his differences from my core; yet, we were a perfect fit. Because never once in those two years was there any doubt that we belonged together.

Yet, after two inseparable and comfortable years, when we returned to the real world, we fell apart with the same alacrity with which we had come together. I worked an eighteen-hour-a-day job in Mumbai, he moved for his second Master's to the States. We didn't even try to make the distance work. We didn't even try to stay friends.

A year later, I saw a picture of him with his newfound love and gave in to demands from my own family to 'settle down'.

I don't know what worked about Rajan—whether it was his good possibility to secure a Green Card or whether it was the fact that his parents were just lovely, so different from mine. They were generous, they were kind, they were supportive and so welcoming. It was a huge contrast from Sahil, who had never bothered introducing me to his.

I didn't see any of the red flags in Rajan. How could I when I met him only a few times? And so his alcoholism and anger issues caught up with us gradually and severely in another continent. He didn't even spare his parents, who cut off ties very soon after. I decided to stay on, trying to make it work—perhaps for myself more than for him, afraid to return to a house that would only shun me. But when I woke up on the floor one summer evening with Rabia crying in the corner and my face soaked in a pool of blood, I realized how stupid I had been. So scared was I for the safety of my child, for losing her to him, being stuck in that foreign land, that I tended not to the knife mark that ran down my face—no stitches, no medical aid, nothing—but instead, I just locked us up and planned our escape.

By the time I reported the case and fled the country, the scar on my face was as permanent as the one in my heart.

And that's why I wore so much make-up.

Giselle

Time: 11.23 p.m.
Unread emails (4,010)

> *'You're fooling no one by pretending to be an involved parent. Also, who are you fooling with those contact lenses?'*

It was ridiculous that I wasn't able to sleep. I was typically so tired that every night, my eyes shut the moment my head hit the pillow.

Yet, here I was, still seething from that judgemental note from Miss Ambika S. Whatever the fuck that 'S' stood for.

We'd sat around, staring at it for a while—the other mums and me. It was surreal that the first five people on her list were exactly the same five people around the table. It almost made me want to question Vidya. Did she copy the teacher's handwriting? Was it some sort of sick teenage joke?

Then Pareeta, of all people, had broken down. I suddenly realized it was true. Pareeta was pregnant. And she hadn't told me. Why? I'd thought we were friends. Close friends!

And this is how I found out? The others had rallied around her as she'd confessed that yes, she was pregnant, but not because she was trying to save her marriage or anything, but I silently scoffed at that. This was totally her trying to save her marriage, if this child was Pankaj's at all. Had she cheated on him? Is that why she hadn't told anyone yet?

There was little time for debate as the others seemed as disturbed by their own personal notes, almost to the point of defiance. It was as if they thought there was some truth in it. To be fair, Pareeta was pregnant and Jia did wear a lot of make-up, and the less we speak about Riddhi's dressing, the better. I, on the other hand, was just furious. How dare she!

We had to complain; I was adamant about that. There was total agreement, except maybe from the mild-mannered Kainaz. Even Pareeta, who is so tender-hearted, agreed immediately. Riddhi took it as far as complaining to the police as she knew the local SP, but I told her we'd start with the principal. We also wondered whether we should tell Rekha Tandon, since she was also mentioned on the sheet, but then thought it would be better to keep it between us. I drafted an email on our behalf, kept it simple asking for time with Mrs Mehta and had hit send before anyone changed their mind.

That was almost a week ago. And now the stupid break had started.

The note tormented me. Day and night. How dare someone judge my parenting style!

Congratulations on your diploma in complaint writing! ...

Constantly raising issues does not make you a better parent ...

I wasn't new to judgement. Earlier, it was my looks. Then it was my attitude. Now, this. I was sick of being slotted by people and taken to trial for who I was.

I was always different. My origins are Anglo-Indian. My great-grandparents were French and had made their home in Pondicherry (now Puducherry), as so many of the migrants had back then. They moved to Mumbai when my mum was in her teens and mum was the first to marry an Indian—a man twelve years her senior, a very well-respected doctor, whose love for his wife and his wine was almost legendary. But also legendary was his daughter, whose tales of rebellion caused ripples in the otherwise quiet neighbourhood of Carmichael Road.

I was forever the talk of class for being fair skinned and brown haired, and for my anglicized English and perfect vocabulary. Since there was no British hangover, I was easily slotted as someone who was conceited and promiscuous, given how easily I attracted the attention of the opposite sex. Initially, it bothered me that I had a reputation even without doing anything. Then they started judging my intelligence—dismissing me as a dumb English girl and as someone who was overtly sexual. My schoolteachers just assumed I was trouble because I was snarkier, smarter, sexier than most; they assumed I was taking favours to get my assignments done or for clearing my exams, and their attitude made me even more defiant and arrogant in my behaviour and ambition. And while more and more people detested my guts, I met the most wonderfully bright and docile Marathi boy who lived down the street and promptly fell in love with him. Rajiv Savarkar was like a whiff of fresh air, much needed for my fiery personality.

His family was well-known for their conservative and orthodox ways and, instinctively dismissed our relationship, just like mine had. Surely I could do better? Surely I could find a better match? Did they not know that you should never tell a rebel what not to do?

We eloped with nothing but a bag full of clothes and a few thousand rupees. We were married in a district court, moved to Delhi and cut off all ties with the families.

It was tough initially—a new city, a new life, a new relationship. We were afraid to even argue with each other because where would we even go if this didn't work out? I worked in a bank to support us, while Rajiv completed his law degree. Then, it was his turn to put his career on pause while I set up my talent management company.

There was no partnership like ours and I would fight a million battles to keep my Rajiv. And we fought a million battles each day with each other, but never against each other because now we knew our relationship was solid enough to endure our outbursts, our failures, our frustrations.

Then along came Kevin, a reminder of a family we had lost and now had the opportunity to build. And when two people start from scratch and establish so much together, they become most protective of their most important asset. And ours was our son.

That's why I was obsessive; I wanted the best in the world for him. I gave him everything I could and pushed him to be the best at everything he did. I gave him exposure to all those five million classes because I *did* want him to have it all. I raised hell for anyone who didn't give it. And I would continue to protect him and fight for him with all my might despite the opinions of people who dared to judge me.

And this bitch had dared to do just that.

Riddhi

Circa: 2001
Weight: 57 kgs
Diet Plan: Chaat. Pakode. Jalebi.

All the chaat-walas in Rajouri knew me. I always got sookhi puri, large-size helping of falooda, gol gappe ka pani and khoya ki barfi to my heart's content—all for free. For two reasons. One, I was with the police. No, no, not like policewoman. I was chief informant and got calls saying 'This has happened, Bhabiji. Do you know?' And I always did know because there wasn't one thing Riddhi Makheeja missed. Aunty Saroj ka necklace case—I saw the boys who were on the motorcycle. Rude letters to Rasika Shivpuri—rude or lewd, I don't know—I just knew who had been following her. Blackmailing Uncle Gaj? I knew which shopkeeper on the street he had a debt with. The police got unsolved case and came running to me for local information. Even now I get 'Happy Birthday, Bhabhi' message every year from SP and all hawaldar bhaiyas.

Which brings me to second reason for being famous: Bhabhi. Ever since I was fifteen, there was not *one* boy who didn't try to line maaro me. When I would walk out of my door in my Karishma Kapoor–style churidaar, just one remark would get one chappal across their face. Nobody dared to come close to flirting with me. And, if it got too much, Harshwardhan Chhabra, who wore two gold chains, one SRK-style 'Cool' bracelet and shoes so pointy they could puncture your tyre, he would turn up with his gang to threaten and make chutney out of the person. He and I were couple since school. I was Punjaban kudi and he was Rajouri ki chhuri.

Why be apologetic for what you are?

We got married at age twenty-one. I got silver bowls set from local police station. I got bail for three local boys in return. I let them off with a warning. But I always knew good from bad. They're all local politicians today and they too send me 'happy b'day, bhabhi' message.

And it is no miracle that genius like Syra was born to us. Harsh didn't go from being salesman to becoming top-level broker in Rajouri and then real estate agent in Gurgaon just like that. I didn't go from being girl who stood on terrace gossiping to becoming police informant to well-networked socialite for nothing. I may not have studied in most hi-fi school but I was the most intelligent girl in my circle. Marks are not the only thing that show intelligence.

So the fact that Miss Ambika thought I was misofeminist was too much!

Your daughter is a delight—mature, smart, curious, kind. But you're almost embarrassed of her excellence. It's always your son you speak of but not of your genius girl. Is there a bit of misogyny you're trying to conceal?

Mysogin. Misogen. I'm not! I have no miss on gender. I believe in woman power the most! I had got Dolly Aunty to expand her boutique. I had financed Rimjhim's divorce lawyer fees. I had made Charul Maasi quit her job when her boss was troubling her. I had stood up for Jia when they had gossiped about her at school. I was the one girls from Rajouri turned to when they had trouble. I was almost like a Lady Don.

And nobody could ever know how proudly I felt about my daughter.

No, I didn't need a stamp from Miss Ambika S.! But now she would get one from me.

Kainaz

So broken was my heart that I couldn't think of any lists. Because while everyone else had vehemently denied theirs, I had accepted mine was true. Of course I hated the city! What was there to love? It was cold and rough, and just teeming with people.

Goa was my home. It was where my friends were, my family was, my life was. It was where I had a business, where I had an identity. I was Kainaz there, not just the wife of Varaz Dotwalla. Goa was where Varaz felt just mine.

A stupid lone tear came rolling down my cheek and I cursed myself for getting unnecessarily emotional. I should have been angry. Maybe I was. Angry at being judged.

I pulled out a table I was working on and then picked up my drill. I was going to bore big, noisy holes into it. It would destroy my beautiful table but it'd be therapeutic. I clipped on my tool belt, put on my protective glasses and was ready to begin. I'd make loads of them. Loads of noisy holes. I hoped they would reverberate down the whole street, the whole market, the whole city! I hoped Miss Ambika would hear it all the way till wherever she lived.

Of course I looked at the city with disdain. Of course I had followed Varaz into the city. Of course I'd heard a thousand times how 'good' Varaz was for me. And he was—he was a lovely, caring human being. And yes, he was a handsome man, a successful actor. But we were partners. We were a couple. We were a team. What had she said in the note that I didn't agree with? Why was it irking me? Was it the tone? Was it the audacity?

I switched on the drill and held it close to the table for a long time. Then I turned it off, unclasped my tool belt and collapsed into my armchair. I *was* making an effort, for the sake of my child, to give this city a chance. I would whisk him as often as possible back to Goa, but I tried not to criticize the city in front of him. I knew he was like a sponge and I didn't want him absorbing any of my negativity. Plus, he enjoyed Gurgaon, much to my dismay. He had friends, he had play dates and he liked Champion Valley School. I couldn't even recall when he'd called his best friend, Roshan, back home last. I knew people looked at me and wondered what sort of celebrity wife was I? A boring one, a badly dressed one, but I didn't care. I shouldn't care. I looked at the table again. I stood up and placed it against the wall, the top facing me. Then I picked up a can of paint and started throwing colours at it. First the darker ones, the red ones, the ones that screamed murder. Then whatever I could get my hands on. Green. Yellow. Black. Gold.

I had followed Varaz blindly into the city. And the city seemed to be blinded by him. Mihir from *We Are the Gondals*. His face was chiselled, his skin ivory and cream, a generous mouth, big, dreamy eyes. The only thing that could be critiqued would be his long nose, which bore a tiny scar from a scuffle years ago, but even that just added to his overall sex appeal. Yes, I was ordinary in comparison but he loved me for me. And I loved him for him. Not for the impact he had on other people, but for the impact he had on me. Right from the first time we'd met.

Ten years ago, Aunty Persis had called me on a Saturday evening asking if we were still looking for tenants for our Panjim apartment.

'My nephew, no, he's got a job with some IT company here. He's looking for a flat and, last time I met your mother, she said your Panaji house was empty. You still looking for a tenant, no?'

So I'd agreed to show him the flat. It had been one of my first few projects. A bare fifth-floor apartment that I'd worked on day and night refurbishing. I'd done a statement wall, I'd done a lovely, textured wallpaper in the bedroom, I'd hand-painted the tiles for the kitchen and I'd made little carvings on the wooden cabinets.

I'd been standing in the living room studying a particular patch in my paintwork, wondering if another coat would suffice or whether I would need more material to smoothen it, when he'd knocked on the open door and asked, 'Hi, can I come in?'

To say that Varaz Dotwalla hadn't had the same effect on me that he has on every other person who liked men would be a lie. He'd stood there in his red-checked shirt and blue jeans, and I thought my knees would buckle and give away. I myself was dressed in a yellow, polka-dotted frock and had my hairband on, looking like the girl from the Amul ad.

I'd stared at him for a minute and he'd stared back at till I'd finally found my bearings.

'You must be Varaz?'

'Yes. Kainaz?'

The difference, Varaz says, was that this time, upon entering the room, he couldn't take his eyes off someone either. Something about me appealed to him—my curly hair, my round twinkling eyes and the way my nose wrinkled when I smiled, or the fact that I was wearing a big frock that screamed Goan girl.

'Do you want to see the house?'

'Um ... Yes, yes, please. Thank you.'

So I'd taken him on a room-by-room tour, trying to keep my eyes on the walls and doors, and not on him. It was almost electrifying and, every time I'd glanced his way, I'd caught him staring at me.

I showed him the view from the balcony, almost itching to move my hand closer to his on the railing. And then we'd stood outside as I'd locked the house followed by a series of politely thank yous—thank you, no, thank *you*, but thank you more—when he'd blurted out, 'Do you want to go out for coffee?'

It was one of those bizarre things. We went on our first date within twenty minutes of meeting each other, kissed twenty-four later and were engaged in two weeks.

Sometime in those two weeks he'd told me he'd done a stint in acting briefly.

'Acted in what?'

'This TV show about five years ago.'

'Oh, so if I Google you, will it show up?'

I sat up from the little picnic rug we were lying on and pulled out my phone. And there it was. *We Are the Gondals*. I had heard of the show but never watched it. Neither had anyone else in my family.

'Why did you leave it?'

'Because I wanted a career. And I didn't like the lifestyle that came with the show.'

'Then why did you do it in the first place?'

He shrugged. 'Youth, I guess. They told me I was good-looking, I should try modelling, make a portfolio, go for a couple of screen auditions and there I was.'

'Can't be as simple as that.'

'I don't know ... I do have it simple in life, I guess. Look at how simply I found you.'

From anyone else, that would look like arrogance. But Varaz was honest and wonderful. I'd realized how kind-hearted and simple he was over the years. And our values were just a perfect match. We liked the same things, wanted the same things and we were so in love. Even after a decade of marriage.

I put the brush down. It made me feel better certainly and no harm had been done. I looked at the table and was slightly taken aback. The splurge of colours had blended with each other, and the golden specks had enhanced the appeal, making it look almost cosmic and ethereal. I walked closer and studied it. I'd call this one 'Expression'. Sometimes, just being able to express yourself was therapy enough, sometimes just throwing out the negativity created something beautiful, sometimes just looking at chaos suddenly showed you opportunity. So intrigued was I that I didn't notice when he entered the workshop.

It was only when he stood behind me, holding me by the waist, his head resting on my shoulder that I leaned back and breathed in the comfortable, gorgeous smell that was truly my Varaz.

'How come you're here?'

He rubbed his nose into my shoulder and took a deep breath. 'K, we need to talk.'

Ambika

The thing was, he hadn't recognized me.
When he had walked into the room on orientation day, everything around us had frozen. I allowed myself to believe, momentarily, that he'd come looking for me—strangely, after all these years—but then he'd looked through me, not a flicker of recognition in his eyes, before he'd calmly walked to the back of the class and joined his beautiful wife.

I'd caught myself in time and it had helped that all the women in class had looked at him with interest too, so I hadn't really stood out as the one gaping at him. But I had avoided his eye after that. Not like he'd ever even hinted at recognizing me. He was an actor after all. Not a great one, mind you, I'd watched *We Are the Gondals* back in the day and bragged to no one in particular: 'Hey, that guy who plays Mihir Gondal? I've shagged him.'

But that was ages ago. Though, technically, he still owed me. I hoped he remembered he owed me.

'Varaz, hi. I mean, Mr Dotwalla, hi. This is Ambika ... Miss Ambika ... Ahaan's class teacher,' I'd introduced myself over the phone.

He'd sounded cautious, wary even. He knew about the note, obviously. Or about me. I could only hope that the angry mums hadn't done anything yet. Mrs Mehta was out of the country for the week, so the meeting was yet to happen.

'Right. I needed some help.' I paused but he didn't say anything. 'I'd like to meet you.' I gripped the phone so tightly that my veins would have gagged and tried to escape my knuckles if they could.

He was quiet for a moment and then asked, 'Why?'

'I'll explain everything when we meet.'

'But what's it about?'

'It's about the ... note.'

'The note?'

'Yes. But I really need to meet you. Today?'

'Today?' he'd asked surprised.

'Yes. 5 p.m.?'

'Um ... I'll just check with my wife and—'

'No! No, I'm so sorry. I *have* to meet you alone. I'm so sorry, I'll explain everything, but I'd really appreciate you not telling your wife about our meeting. Once again, I'm sorry, I know how that sounds and feel free to tell her everything afterwards. That's up to you, but I really need to speak to you alone.'

There was silence and I could imagine how crazy this sounded, but what about this situation wasn't?

'And it can't be done over the phone?'

'It's best done in person.'

He didn't say anything for a bit. 'I do want you to know that I will be telling Kainaz about this meeting,' he warned me.

'Sure. But I don't want her to be there just this once. Look, we'll meet at a public place and I'll explain.'

'I—'

'Just fifteen minutes. Then your wife can join us if you like.'

He was quiet for a moment but then, thankfully, agreed. We decided upon a café near his workplace and I sincerely hoped not to bump into any of my students—or worse, their parents. I dressed down, wore an oversized shirt, dropped all my makeup and sat with my sunglasses on, a baseball cap covering my mop of hair. I received a lot of strange glances and perhaps my disguise attracted more attention than I had planned.

He arrived ten minutes late, bringing the whole café to a halt with his enigmatic presence and scanned the room. He looked past me—not once, but twice!—and I understood, with foreboding, that he really *didn't* recognize me. I raised my hand and beckoned him over.

'Miss Ambika?' he asked with a curious frown upon his face and I waved him to sit down maintaining a cordial smile that did not mirror the absolute shipwreck I was feeling inside.

'So glad you could make it. Coffee?' I asked.

'I'll get it. Can I get you something?'

I tapped my tall glass of iced tea and I wished it were the long-island version, but I needed to hold on to all my senses to be able to have this conversation. I was also glad he wasn't hostile and still had his manners about him, so hopefully this would go better than expected ...

Or not.

What was I thinking? I'd written such mean things about his wife!

He came back with a cup of cappuccino for himself and even bought me a muffin. Maybe he was being a gentleman, maybe he was being nice because I was still his son's class teacher. Or maybe he *did* recognize me after all, because I remember him studying me a bit too long at the PTM, almost like he were trying to place me in his memory. Well, he'd know soon enough.

'Right,' I started and then felt a bulldozer of nerves roll over me. I swallowed hard and cleared my throat. I took off my sunglasses and my cap, and looked him straight in the eye.

'Do you know who I am?'

He looked surprised. 'Aren't you Miss Ambika?'

'Yes ... but anything else?'

'Um ...'

'Do you remember meeting me?'

'At the PTM?'

'No, I meant before school.'

'Uh ... the orientation?'

Fuck.

'I'll give you another hint,' I tried. 'Do you remember Berlin, 2007?'

He blinked at me, trying to fit in all the pieces in the puzzle, and suddenly his eyes grew wide. Thank god they went wide because as the horror of recognition dawned upon him, I saw a sliver of hope.

'But that was ... Was that ... But that was ...'

To be fair, I looked different then. I was carrying oodles of teenage weight, my frizzy hair touched my waistline, statement frames covered half my face, my teeth not yet been Invisaligned and I had a mole on my chin that I hadn't yet lasered down to a beauty spot.

I was eighteen. India still had the DDLJ hangover but not the ZNMD phase yet. So, in a way, we were pioneers. We'd packed our bags and headed out for a Euro trip—the six of us. We'd done Milan, Prague, Budapest and turned up at Berlin fifteen days later. After sufficient amounts of sightseeing, shopping and rave partying, my friends announced they were heading to one of Berlin's famous weekly street food events. I'd taken a quick shower, pulled on a nice, short georgette floral dress, hung a cross-body sling bag across my chest and followed them out.

The event was crazy from the word go. There were so many people, so much food, such a vast variety of colour, sounds and smells that I felt completely intoxicated and excited. It was like a high-end Kumbh Mela, igniting all the senses, pulling us in different directions. The area was dotted with stalls, there was a large sitting area—much like a food court—and the variety of food was mind-boggling. I abandoned my lot and headed in search for a curry. I hadn't dared to admit that I was missing Indian food already, it would make me so uncool. So I'd walked the entire expanse before landing up at a not-so-creatively named stall called 'Khana Khazana: The Taste of India'.

'I'll have a thaali,' I placed my order. It was while waiting for my tray that I noticed the customer next to me. He was leaner than he was now, had a little spot of acne around his prominent cheeks, his hair was curly and long enough to reach his shoulders, and he wore a dark-blue bucket hat. He could have been from anywhere across the world, given his shiny

ivory skin, and he looked at me and gave me a brief smile while we waited in silence for our orders.

In my head, I debated a million opening lines and conversation starters, but none of them made it to my tongue. His food arrived quicker than mine and he left, weaving through the crowd.

I almost snatched the tray when my order made an appearance and scanned the crowd for him. Fortunately, he was sitting alone, concentrating on his biryani. I walked as fast as I could without letting my papad do a runner. But just before I could reach his table, a very sexy girl in a very sexy leather skirt that barely covered her very sexy bum asked him if the seat was taken. He shook his head, so she planted herself there as I watched on in pure lust and disappointment. For a brief second, or maybe it was my imagination, I saw him glance over at me as I sat a few seats away from them. They started chatting—who wouldn't?—and I heard snatches of their conversation.

'I'm Tish ... traveling with friends ... love it here... Russia.'

Tish with a great tush, I thought to myself grudgingly as he listened to her intently, concentrating on his food. He said something in a low voice and I strained my ears, but couldn't hear anything over the chaos of the hall. Till a word jumped out and smacked me.

'India.'

India! My head jerked up and my heart started banging in my chest.

'Mumbai ... student ... two years in London ...'

I wanted to dance with delight! In my head, we were already married by virtue of sharing the same ethnicity. I wanted to scream, 'So am I! So am I! I am also Indian!' and elbow sexy Tish with the great tush out to establish ownership, but she wasn't giving up. You could see it in her fluttering eyelashes and suggestive body language.

I turned back grumpily to my plate. It lost all signs of being appetizing. The pulao was more like khichdi, the butter paneer was just that—butter and paneer with no other flavour—the mixed vegetable turned out to be broccoli and pumpkin—ugh!—and the papad had gone from being Superman to SpongeBob. I tore a piece of the elastic naan and chewed on it unhappily before giving up.

It was then that I heard raised voices. A burly, bulky man covered in tattoos had landed up by sexy Tish's side. They spoke in Russian. I was good with languages. I'd learnt Russian when I was twelve, though I did find it rather hard to read.

'Where have you been?' big burly asked sexy Tish-tush angrily.

'What's it to you?'

She flashed a smile at her Indian partner and steered the hulk away to the side. I sensed drama so I kept my ears trained on their conversation.

'Who is that?'

'None of your business!'

'You've been avoiding me on purpose!'

'Of course, I have! You're suffocating me, following me everywhere!'

'We're going home.'

'We're not! Let go of me, you fucking bully!'

'Are you going home with him then? Because if you are, I'll break his nose!'

'Fuck off, Alex!' She pulled herself taller to stand nose-to-nose against him and I had to admire her guts. 'You touch him and I'll break your nose!'

She spun around on her very high heels and stalked off, just as the giant turned to glare in the direction of the Indian guy, who was licking off the last of his raita, oblivious to the drama he had caused.

'Who is he?' I took a peek to see that a friend had joined the giant.

'Some bloke Tish seems to have taken a shining to. Did you see them chatting at the table? I could see her undressing him with her eyes.'

'Ah, these German men! We should have never come!'

'He's not German. He fucking Indian. I'm going to show him what he gets for hitting on my girl!'

I don't know what made me do it, maybe it was solidarity because he was my countryman, maybe because of the way he had looked at me before she'd taken the seat next to him, maybe the fact that I'd felt my heart flutter to my mouth when I'd seen him, but I quickly found my way to his seat, as the crowd got thicker and held him by the elbow feeling very panicked.

'We have to go,' I said, my voice low and urgent.

He looked at me in confusion. 'Sorry, what?'

A group of students had now started milling about and I saw this as an opportunity to lose our tail.

'I have no time to explain but we have to get out, now!'

'Do you have the wrong—'

'Now! Go, go, go!'

Maybe it was the urgency in my voice or maybe he saw the giant walking towards us, but he picked up his bag, and allowed me to hold his hand and run. We zig-zagged across the tables, around people, escaping many a precarious tray, walking faster and faster till we reached the exit. Then we made a run for it, turning the corner, running down the street and creating as much distance between us and the food festival. We stopped at a darkened alley, panting.

'Do you mind,' he asked breathlessly, 'explaining what that was all about?'

That's when I realized I may have made a mistake. 'Oh shit! Did you know that girl?'

'What girl?'

'The girl in the leather skirt.'

'Leather skirt?'

'The one who was sitting next to you at the table right now. Tish. Tush.'

'The Russian? No, she was just friendly.' Then his eyes widened in disbelief. 'Was she a spy?'

I was dumbstruck. 'A spy? Why would you think she's a spy?'

He looked sheepish. 'Too many novels?'

'Well, I don't know who she was but I just overheard her boyfriend acting very jealous and threatening to break your nose for talking to her.'

'What?' He gave me the same look Dodo gave me often. The are you crazy look. I ignored it.

'Look, they were talking in Russian. I speak it. I could understand them.'

Suddenly his whole body language changed, he looked at me doubtfully, perhaps wondering if I was a nutcase, because, hello, that's how I sounded. I flushed, realizing how lame I sounded now as he straightened up and cleared his throat.

'Right. Er ... thanks for the warning but I don't even know her, or him, for that matter. So I guess I'll be okay. Maybe he was just a jealous boyfriend.'

'Yes,' I said collecting myself too. 'Of course. Sure.'

We stood in awkward silence then, me wanting to die in shame and him nodding politely.

'Thanks, then. I'll see you around.'

'I'll see you around.'

Of course, neither of us was really 'seeing' anything because, out of nowhere, a fist came pumping through the air and broke the Indian guy's beautiful aquiline nose. I stood in shock as he doubled over in pain and fell to the ground, and, just then, the girl in the leather skirt appeared behind the giant, flipped him around and punched him straight in the face too.

'You fuck face, Alex, take that for getting in my way! We're over!'

She turned on her heel and stomped off, the giant suddenly turning into a pathetic little mouse, holding his punctured cheek and racing after her with a string of apologies. And then I heard him groan, his hand clutching his nose, blood all over his face.

'Shit!' I knelt down beside him. 'We'd better get you to a hospital.'

'Eh ... no. I don't have insurance. I'll be okay.'

'But you're hurt!'

He didn't say anything, so I looked around for help, people pouring out of pubs and restaurants, nobody seeming to have noticed us. I dug into my bag and passed him a pack of tissues that he immediately pressed against his nose.

'Look,' I offered, 'I'm staying just down the block from here. Why don't you come and clean up?'

'No, you've already been so helpful. I can't—'

'You look a wreck! You need to ice that, like, now!'

He was obviously in a lot of pain because he nodded and murmured 'thanks'. I helped him up and led him down the street.

'I'm sorry I should have paid more attention to what you were saying,' he mumbled.

'I'm sorry I didn't see him come out of the blue … Or darkness … Or whatever.'

I think he smiled but he had too much tissue covering his face.

'I'm Varaz,' he said.

'Mira.'

Lesson Eleven
Philosophy

From: Grade Coordinator Shilpa Anand <Shilpa.anand@cvs.in>
To: III B Parents Group
Date: 10 October 2022 at 9:00 AM
Sub: Regarding Class Teacher

Dear Parents,

Stephen Hawking wisely said, '*Intelligence is the ability to adapt to change.*'

We regret to inform you that Miss Ambika has taken ill and will be on leave next week. In the meantime, we will do our very best to ensure that no learning is paused for the children. Substitute teachers have been assigned and they will help children finalize their goals for the next term. We will also dive into the second-term syllabus with as much enthusiastic rigour as we had at the start of the year.

Please feel free to reach out to me directly in the absence of Miss Ambika. We wish her a speedy recovery and look forward to welcoming her back post the Diwali break.

Warmest regards,

Shilpa Anand
Coordinator, Grades III, IV & V

Jia

> Jia, did you hear from Mrs Mehta?

> Yes. She's back from her vacation but has fallen sick

> As has their class teacher conveniently!

> Ok.

> Rabia's come home with three notes in her diary

> Why?

> Unsharpened pencils, unhealthy tiffin box, talking out of turn

> That's strange.

> Is she upset?

> She's upset that Miss Ambika's on leave

> Forced leave soon

> Some new teacher took class. Can you talk?

> Since Giselle has mailed them five times already

Will you?

> No. We'll meet in person.

Syra called. Said they have three tests next week

> But it's holiday time

New term I guess?

> Mom, can you instead cancel the dentist?
>
> Going to Kainaz's house

> No, I'm in a meeting

> Why?

Nothing. She sounded unhappy. Call her

> She'll get used to it

Unsharpened pencils is a bit too much to warrant a note?

Yes. They've been given a lot of homework too

> Really?

> But they never do during holidays

According to Rabia the substitute teacher was very strict

> What rubbish!

Well, Rabia is imitating her

You may want to take it up with the principal when you meet her?

> Wait, I just got an email from the principal's office

What does it say?

> Hang on

They want to know if they can fix up a virtual call

Giselle

Time: 3.30 p.m.
Unread emails (3,150)

What the *fuck* just happened?
Why did we agree to this? What sort of negotiation will we have? How can they even think of it?

I didn't care if it was the right thing to do. I didn't care if we could gain something out of this. I didn't even care if what she'd written was the truth! It was the *audacity* she had to write it. To sit on a high horse and judge our parenting styles, when she has no children of her own!

Why were we even agreeing to grant this crazy lady an audience?

I had vehemently opposed it on the group and had given Pareeta a mouthful when she'd called. But some sort of maternal love seems to be flowing through her system, and she wants to be generous with a woman who has been nothing but vicious and irresponsible.

Then Kainaz had called me to convince me, but I told them I wouldn't spend a second over fifteen minutes in a room with that woman. Bloody bitch!

I wanted Rajiv to come for the goddamn meeting but Pareeta said it's best if we the mums do it. What's with this 'we the mums' shit? It's because her stupid, rotten Pankaj does nothing. I'm pretty sure he hasn't even done anything to get Pareeta pregnant. She must be virgin mother Mary. Rajiv told me it was none of my business but I thought of Pareeta as a sister and was hurt that she hadn't bothered telling me. Especially when you could see the sadness in her eyes. Why should anyone feel sad and apologetic about their pregnancy?

They're all the same. They're not my friends. They're just mums of Champion Valley School. Acquaintances, at best. I didn't know who I was angrier with—Miss Ambika for writing such shit or Pareeta for keeping the truth from me. How could she think I would judge her? I was her *friend*; I don't have it in me to judge anyone!

But now, I wouldn't be surprised if the teacher was right. That Pareeta was having this baby to save her marriage. Why would she want to save a marriage with that nincompoop of a man was beyond me. He was never around. Never! Yet, I was the absentee parent as per Miss Ambika. It was always the mothers who got all the blame.

Why, oh why, were we listening to her apology? Why couldn't we just let the authorities sort it out with her? No, I wasn't going to let that lot tell me what to do. I'd listened to them enough.

I clicked on compose email and started to type.

Dear Principal Mehta ...

I didn't know how to start, so I sat there trying to focus. What was the moot point? That one of her staff members had dared to say something about the parents? Or *what* she had to say about the parents? It was a bit of both, I decided.

This is regarding the teacher Miss Ambika S.

I paused and something didn't look right. What was it? There was something missing in my mind map. I shook my head and continued. The words suddenly flowed out of me.

I assassinated her character single-handedly. What were her credentials? Where had she taught before? She lacked confidence, looked confused in our interactions and clearly had too much free time to be writing such notes. She was much too young, too inexperienced, too dispassionate about her job, because who dares to speak to parents about their parenting capabilities! How dare she make us sound like we're out of an OTT show? *The Fabulous Lives of Mums*! As if all we did was sit around sipping our margheritas, asking the village to raise our children. Try being one of us for a day, Miss Ambika S.!

We wanted her out of the system, I demanded. We wanted it to go on her record so that she never took us parents for granted. She was unfit for this position here as well as anywhere else. She had no empathy, no integrity, no humanity. We wanted her punished and dismissed immediately. Nothing less would do.

But as my cursor hovered around the send button, Rajiv's voice suddenly appeared by my side.

'Sounds like you're judging her too.'

'What?'

'You're judging her. You're also judging the other mums. You're all constantly judging each other.'

Fuck you, Rajiv! I seethed, but instead simply said, 'Stop reading my emails.'

I slammed my laptop shut and stood up to leave.

'Where are you going?'

'I have to meet the mums.'

I took my bag, put on my jacket and was about to slam the door shut when he said, 'Gis, aren't you forgetting something again?'

Good god! Did he really want a kiss in the mood I was in? After what he'd said to me! I stared at him and he raised his eyebrows. Then I remembered. My green contact lenses. The ones Miss Ambika had caught me out on.

Kainaz

	A list of the most daring things I have done in life:
1.	Married a man I knew in less than a month
2.	Delivered a baby without an epidural
3.	Bungee jumping in Thailand
4.	Rolled a joint under the table sitting across from my father-in-law
5.	Pretended to be a stripper to gain entry into a very private nightclub
6.	Decided to play mediator between a group of very disgruntled mums and a woman who had once slept with my husband. Yes, happening now

I had tried not to laugh but I had. I should have been horrified and jealous, instead something about the panic in his eyes made me laugh.

'Miss Ambika? She's the girl from Berlin?'

He nodded.

'The time you got that scar on your nose?'

'Yes.'

'The one who told you to start modelling?'

'Yes.'

'The one-night stand?'

He sighed. 'Yes.'

'The one you left even without a note the morning after?'

'Yes.'

'And you didn't recognize her?'

'No. She was chubbier then, more … hippie. She didn't have this accent.'

'But, you told me her name was—'

'It is.'

I tried to remember everything else he had told me and then it struck me. 'Oh my god. Varaz, does she …'

'Yes. She does. I didn't know. I didn't know till now. Sit down, K.'

I sat in the chair. Fifteen years or whatever, but how can you forget who you had slept with? Of course Varaz was a celebrity and had been with many women in those days, but to *forget* what they looked like?

'So now what?' I'd asked finally.

'Well … I owe her. She really did help me that evening with my broken nose and … everything.'

I raised an eyebrow. 'Everything?'

'You know how it is.'

'What is she asking of you now?'

'Simply to grant her a window to apologize.'

'Simply?'

'Plus, you know … Do we want to say no to someone like her?'

The mums had been horrified when I'd asked them to come over so that Miss Ambika could meet us. Though what explanation would hold good with four very angry women was very difficult to foresee. I say four and not five because somewhere in that paint flinging, perhaps I could see her point. I was too disdainful of the city. I was letting it impact Ahaan. I had to set it right.

'Thank you so much for doing this,' Miss Ambika had said, her eyebrows knit in anguish as she'd reached my house. She looked very unlike her glamorous self at school. She was in jeans and sneakers, her hair frizzy and her face free of any make-up.

I gently closed the door behind her.

'I've only promised you an audience. I can't do anything else.' I didn't know whether to be polite or curt. I'd actually only wanted to pat her on her shoulder comfortingly knowing the other mums would rip into her.

'Are they here?' Miss Ambika asked timidly, pulling off her sneakers in the corner. Her voice sounded more high-pitched than I'd ever heard before.

'Pareeta, Aryan's mother, is here.'

There was a flash of relief on her face. Pareeta was more kindly than the others and I could almost imagine her crumbling if I had said Giselle was here.

Varaz walked into the hallway and stopped awkwardly.

'Hi.'

'Hi. Thank you so much for doing this.'

He nodded. 'Uh, I won't be sitting in for your... conversation. And I also just want you to know that Kainaz ... er ... knows. About Berlin, I mean.'

To her credit, she didn't look worried. Rather, she looked impressed and relieved. 'Well it was just a—'

'She also knows,' Varaz said, 'um ... who you are.'

Ambika frowned a little. 'Oh. Um ... yes, but I'd really appreciate it if we didn't talk about that. That has no bearing whatsoever on ...'

I studied her, my head bursting with questions but I didn't ask. I simply nodded and led her to the living room. Pareeta was admiring the carved mirror I'd just finished.

'This is so pretty, Kainaz. It must've taken you ages to make it!' Then she spotted Ambika and stiffened.

'Mrs Singh,' Ambika said faux cheerfully. 'So nice to meet you. Thank you for meeting me.'

Pareeta frowned, almost uncomfortably.

'I'm only doing this because Kainaz says we should give you a chance to explain yourself. But I cannot promise a favourable outcome, I'm sorry.'

She turned back to the mirror, her mind no longer on the design.

We sat in silence until Riddhi and Jia walked in, and Varaz offered to take the children down to the park. The two ladies were immediately taken in by how my house looked, I could tell, by the way they scanned the room for furniture and I allowed myself to feel a spot of pride but, before they could say anything, they noticed Ambika and there was deathly silence.

Everyone sat around, the tension palpable, and I served tea, checking my phone again and again to see if Giselle had indeed stood us up. But then, half an hour later, she breezed in, barking into her phone, showing no courtesy of removing her shoes as the others had at the doorstep, nodding 'hello' at all of us but ignoring Miss Ambika completely. Then, without apology, she planted herself in the centre of the room, as if she was here to chair the meeting while the rest of us meekly squeezed ourselves on the sofa.

'I have to leave in fifteen minutes,' she announced and then pierced Miss Ambika with her cat-green eyes. 'Begin.'

Riddhi

Weight: 50/60/70/80 ... Who cares?
Diet Plan: Fingernails, mostly

But what she could say to make better? All the basic sorry-sorry, made mistake, don't think like that ... It was total drama! Not the Netflix ones, unless you're thinking *Sacred Games* vibes, but the ones that air on cable TV—*Naagin* variety. The ones Mummy watches with so much glee, where they make her believe that big fat joint families are the best, that maa is always very bechari, that bahus only purpose in life is to come between mother and son, and it gives her reason to keep my brother and poor bhabi in her house under her nose.

Anyway, this was worse than that!

I thought so that Miss Ambika would be more nervous but she looked quite calm for someone who was meeting a pack of wolves—matlab, us angry mamas. She apologized sincerely and all, but I was in no mood to be kind. I toh turned my nose up and looked at my nails only like I'd decided to do. They show that in serials: If you want to show you have too much attitude, you look at your nails.

So I did that. I had told Jia also in the car to be snooty and not very nice but she was actually looking like she was listening to Miss Ambika and that irritated me. I had to kick her one-two times so that she could also show some attitude. And maybe she was, par itne layers of make-up mein, one can barely see.

Miss Ambika was right about Jia though. She's my bestie but her make-up is too much cake-up. I made a note to buy some La Prairie skin products for her. Pata hi nahin chalta make-up kiya hai! It's so good I couldn't tell my cleaning woman had been using my make-up quietly for months. I just thought she's glowing too much! Must be having affair with cook. Then one day I saw half bottle finished and then she was finished. I got her new make-up box and said you use this instead of finishing my bottles. I was also happy it was just make-up and not affair with cook because he has all these affairs and then maids run away.

Anyway, Giselle Savarkar toh gave her a mouthful only. Not my maid. Miss Ambika. She heard all the sorry-sorry that Miss Ambika was showering then asked her important question: Why us mummys only? Why not daddys? Which was right. I know I dress OTT but Harsh toh looks like he's a disco ball and she had said nothing about him. And why did she say Pareetaji was trying to save her marriage? People have different ways of saving marriage, so maybe getting pregnant was hers. I also saved my marriage by making sure Harsh's sisters lived far away in Pitampura. I swear they call me bhabi-bhabi but I tolerate them only for my husband.

Anyway, Giselle Savarkar is so feminine—or feminist or whatever—she kept saying this is the problem with people, women bring down women, we only have to bring up children, fathers don't take any blame, we only have issues, such a misogen-something society. And I toh agreed with all my heart because Miss Ambika had used that term for *me*! I had toh started feeling so guilty that when I bought Shivam a NERF last week—I think so we can start an army with the number of NERFs we have now—I got one for Syra also out of guilt. Syra told me that Mama, but I don't play with guns and don't endorse it either! So I told her, haan, but I'm not asking you to do advertisement, no? Just play with it. I have to do things equal-equal for both my children. Else people say I only prefer Shivam.

Anyway, I got little upset ki only Giselle is handling meeting so I also loudly said, 'We mothers only do all the work. Then we only get all the laanat!' Kainaz looked at me blankly and her Hindi is a bit weak so I explained, "Laanat" means we only get kicked. But why us? Why us five only? Also Rekha Tandon but she's toh crack only. Why not that Amrita–Amruta? Their Kieras and Kairas are so badly brought up, they always make fun of my Syra for being intelligent. Unka kyun nahin likha?' I nudged Jia to speak. 'You also say, Jia!'

'I agree,' Jia agreed like a good girl. 'Why did you zero in on us to begin with? There are so many more obvious examples of bad parenting. There's this woman, I can't remember her name, her daughter was super friendly when we moved here first but when I met the mum, either she had a problem with me being a single mum or she thought I was some sort of plebian and stopped talking to us.'

I nodded encouragingly even though I wanted to tell her it's 'lesbian' not 'plebeian'.

'What about the lady whose son has long hair?' Pareeta asked, as if getting encouraged by us. 'He uses such foul language! I've even heard the parents use foul language indiscriminatingly around our children!'

And then, Giselle again seeking attention, said, 'And that horrible lady who sent out birthday invites to everyone but us! Despite me going out of my way to make her feel welcome at Kevin's birthday.'

Uff! Giselle also is bit much. Uska out of the way is so in the way. When I had come with Syra for Kevin's last birthday, she had told me, thank you, you can pick her up in two hours. Matlab main kya blow dry karake gaadi mein baithne gayi thi? She should have said birthday party only for children on invite! I wouldn't have wasted an outfit. And she didn't even ask us for cake when we went to pick up children. And the cake was plain chocolate. Not even theme.

I looked up at Kainaz but she had nothing to say. I couldn't understand. She didn't have problem with other mothers? Then she cleared her throat.

'But aren't we doing what Miss Ambika did? Aren't *we* also being nasty about other mums? None of us have mentioned the dads.'

'I'll mention a dad!' Giselle piped up again. 'Arush something. He's always passing snide comments. Like, on orientation day, he called me "Loki"! I mean, what was that all about?'

I wanted to tell her he probably meant lauki because she really did look like the vegetable that day in her green business suit but didn't say anything. Because I think so we're all friends now, we have our own WhatsApp group so we don't bitch about each other at least.

'The point is,' Kainaz said reasonably, 'I think we all have a tendency to judge other people—we even judge each other as friends. So maybe we can give Miss Ambika a second chance.'

Suddenly I got suspicious of Kainaz's behaviour. The *Jab We Met* scene came rushing into my head. When Kareena had said, 'Chakkar kya hai, boss?' That's what I wanted to ask Kainaz. Why she was so keen on forgiving? I raised my eyebrows at Jia and then even caught Pareeta looking confused.

Miss Ambika rubbed her face in embarrassment. 'I'm so sorry. I know how hurtful it is but it was by sheer coincidence that I wrote about the some of you, you five in particular as your children sit together in class, so in my head they're one team. And I was having a bad day and I would have probably gone on to write about the other parents as well which doesn't justify anything. But I'm really, really sorry. To be fair, it was my personal thoughts on you—not on your children. I'm just so fond of them. They're literally my favourites.'

Bhai, bade dramebaaz hai! If this is how she treats favourites, imagine non-favourites?

'The thing is, I don't even know you guys. I'm just stupidly basing my opinion on my interaction with your kids. And of course, you're all great mums, great parents! I'm just ... Those were just my stupid private thoughts.'

'They stopped being private when you wrote them down!' Giselle said sounding just like vamp from *Sasural Simar Ka*. 'What if our children had found it instead of us? They can read. How do you think it would make them feel?'

Hain! Her Kevin can read so much? Syra toh says teacher is always telling him read more, improve more.

'Look, I'm so sorry about what I've done,' Miss Ambika went on. 'I'm here to beg for your forgiveness. There is no excuse and even though you weren't meant to see it, I should not have even said anything. I know that if you bring this up with Mrs Mehta, I will lose my job. Rightly so. But I really don't want to lose my job. I *can't*. I *really*, really can't. Please!'

She actually folded her hands. Like a beggar! My soft heart melted only. Gareeb hai shayad bechari. I felt bad because she'll lose job and losing job is not easy but suspension toh banta hai. But knowing khaddoos Mrs Mehta, she will toh kick her out of her job. I only wanted her suspended. It's true. I started having second thoughts. I think so for a moment others did too.

But then Giselle, and you can trust her to say something always, she turned to Kainaz and asked her straight off, 'What is your deal? Come clean. Why did *you* orchestrate this meeting? Why are you on her side?'

I wanted to say orchestra ka stick toh Giselle only moved given how she moderated our session but Kainaz took a deep breath.

'Varaz and Ambika turned out to be old friends. They'd known each other briefly in Germany and, even though we only recently discovered that, Ambika did reach out asking for an audience with us and I thought it's only fair we grant it.'

'But why?' Giselle cried. I agreed with her. Why? What do we owe her?

'Because, I feel like even though it wasn't very nice of her to say it, she was telling the truth, wasn't she? I mean, I don't know about you but I do dislike Gurgaon a lot and I am letting that prejudice seep through to Ahaan, and that's not a nice thing to do. So maybe it's the bitter truth, but it's the truth, even if it's been told bitterly.'

I think so even she got confused by what she was saying but we all kept quiet because it was true that Pareeta was saving marriage and Jia did wear too much make-up and *hai*! Socha hi nahin but Giselle wears contact lenses? Like *Baazigar* ka Shah Rukh Khan?

Before I could think what that meant and whether she was also murderess like SRK in the movie, the door opened and the children came in from the park with super hunk husband of Kainaz. And while I admit I couldn't make my eyeballs unfreeze from the outline of his jaw—hai, kya soch ke banaya hai bhagwan ne—there was some activity in the background that I almost missed. When I did turn, I saw the children going mad, hugging Miss Ambika. They toh acted like pata nahin who has come to the house. Like Shivam would feel if he ever met Blippi.

My heart toh became wet cloth as if nichod diya gaya ho. So badly it felt squeezed that they were hugging traitor who said such bad-bad things about them. Then I realized that she didn't say bad things about any of them—only about us. Unki toh she is favourite. And, as per her, they're her favourites.

How will our children feel if we get their favourite teacher suspended?

Lesson Twelve
Moral Science

From: Grade Coordinator Shilpa Anand <Shilpa.anand@cvs.in>
To: happyriddhi@tmail.com, Giselle.savarkar@hirearchy.com, Jia@avstech.com, pareetaspastries@tmail.com, kainaz.dotwalla@tmail.com
Date: 25 October 2022 at 10:12 AM
Sub: Request for meeting

Dear Parents,

'Turn your wounds into wisdom'- Oprah Winfrey

As you might know, Mrs Mehta is down with a severe viral infection. We are sorry to have postponed the meeting for two weeks now. If you'd like, we could set up a meeting with the vice-principal or if there's any way I can be of assistance, do let me know. Else, we will set it up first thing after the break.

Wishing you all a very happy Diwali!

Regards,

Shilpa Anand
Coordinator, Grades III, IV & V

Ambika

Dodo sat opposite me as I buried my head in my arms. I knew he was trying not to smile.

'So, basically you stayed out of trouble for exactly six months.'

'Record-breaking,' I said sarcastically but felt like a boulder had been roped to my heart and I was sinking faster than the Titanic.

'Mrs Mehta's going to flip,' he commented as if that would be news to me.

I churned out a freshly wounded groan for his benefit. 'What can I even do now?'

'Get a new job?'

I looked up. 'You're right. NASA did send me an offer letter.'

'I'm serious.'

'So am I. They're sending some mission to the moon in a few years. Maybe I'd be good for something on another planet.'

'The moon isn't a planet.'

'No shit. See why I suck at being a teacher?'

'You could revert to plan B and marry rich.'

'I couldn't do that to you.'

'I do have a healthy bank balance now.'

'Yet, all I got from your six months in Australia was a keychain.'

'I thought it was sweet! A little home keychain for your new home.'

'For *your* home!'

'If it were my home, we would have a little more furniture around the house.'

I looked around at the strewn floor cushions, a bean bag and a badly covered mattress.

'You should've rented me a fully furnished flat.'

'I didn't know you'd want to move in overnight. Anyway, I'm very impressed that I receive the rent on time every month.'

'You can return it all now that I'll have no job.'

He put his hand on my knee. I shoved it off.

'Don't be so hard on yourself. You want another beer?'

'Do you think this has ever happened before?'

He rolled his eyes. 'Mira, I don't think this or anything else like this has happened in any school anywhere across the globe!'

'No ... I meant have they ever fired a teacher before at CVS?'

'Not that I know of. And why would I know of such things? Why don't you ask Mrs Mehta?'

I was too tired to even want to slap him. 'How did that report card get there? I wasn't so stupid that I would leave it lying around.' Yet, clearly, I was stupid enough to have written it.

Dodo frowned. 'Where had you kept it?'

I tried to think back to the day. 'It was in my drawer. Or something.'

He placed a hand on my shoulder and I knew the look in his eye but didn't really want to acknowledge it. 'You're not the most organized person though ...'

'I thrive in chaos,' I admitted as I once again scanned the room and realized that indeed it did look unkempt—there were takeout boxes lying in a corner when Dodo had arrived and he had spent ten minutes straightening out the books lying on the floor. And there was a lot of paper so ...

I sighed. 'Okay so maybe it was lying around on my table somewhere, but it certainly wasn't mixed up with the report cards. And then I dropped everything when I saw the golden saree Syra's mum was wearing ...' I groaned again.

'You know, Mira, how about not writing some of these things next time?'

'Do you think they'll forgive me?'

'I don't know them to be able to answer that.'

'Would *you* forgive me?'

He shrugged. 'Sure. But I could be biased because I'm in love with you.'

I threw a cushion at him. 'Fuck off. Why are you even here? It's the night before Diwali! You should be at one of those fancy card parties in the farmhouse area.'

'What and miss out on all this drama? What's your plan for tomorrow?'

'I'm not going home if that's what you're asking.'

'Mira ...'

'I'm serious. And no, I'm not going to yours either before you ask.'

'But it's Diwali. You can't just sit around here and sulk!'

'A girl's got to do what a girl's got to do!'

'I'm having none of this. You're either going to your place or my place, and that's final.'

I couldn't help breaking out into a grin. 'Mi casa, su casa has a whole new meaning!'

He shook his head and walked to the kitchen to fetch more beer just as his phone pinged. Email alert. I would have ignored had it not held a familiar name.

Giselle Savarkar.

Giselle

Time: 8.25 p.m.
Unread emails (2,300)

I've run a talent management firm for fourteen years. We call ourselves head-hunters but actually, people hunt for us. People catch hold of me at the strangest of places because they feel like I'm going to be that catalyst that will help them take a leap in their career. I was accosted at the salon once, my hair all over my face, my hairdresser lecturing me on how to hydrate it better with argan oil when someone had crept behind me and shoved her phone in my face and said, 'Can you take a look at my CV? I was wondering if it sounds good enough? Ajit here told me you're a head-hunter and I am so glad I caught you at a good time.' So I'd glared at her and she'd said, 'I mean good time for me, not for you, of course, because your hair really does need hydration but here you go!' I had stomped into the office and made sure we struck her off all our databases.

Once I'd been cycling with our group—many years ago, when I still had the luxury of time and was eager to lose my pregnancy weight—when a man had glided up to me and said, 'Rajiv said you're a head-hunter. I'm looking to upskill. Can you guide me?' I sped away so fast that the only skill he could have immediately upped was his speed.

I have met people bursting with talent and not making it anywhere, and the most untalented ones racing up the ladder but the reason I was suddenly thinking about talent—mind maps—was because after the pre-Diwali party downstairs in the lawns, I realized my beloved son Kevin didn't have any. He spent two thousand rupees trying to win a bar of chocolate and the organizer had finally given him one out of pity. He'd lost every single game he played.

You would think someone who had been playing football for years would have better focus and aim, but he kept sticking his tongue out and throwing the ring into the bin. At first, Rajiv and I laughed and took pictures, but, by the end of it, I was convinced he needed a visit to the optometrist.

Diwali melas pained me. They were too bright, too loud, too crowded. I had no intention of attending it to blend in with the women in lehengas swirling in every colour possible, dripping with fake jewellery, making random conversation and dancing to loud, cackling music. But then Pareeta had messaged.

> Will you guys be going down? I can take Kevin with me, if you like. I have to leave at 8 for a family dinner, so can drop him off before that.

Rajiv announced he would take him and I told him to go ahead, sitting myself at my work desk and shutting all the windows to keep the mayhem out. But then Miss Ambika's note came floating back into my head—the jibe at my sheer pretence of being an involved parent. So I took it upon myself to prove her wrong.

I received quite a few curious glances, perhaps because I was in jeans while everyone else all with bling, but Kevin was thrilled to have me by his side. He squeezed my hand and skipped along the periphery, waving to everyone in general.

'Do you really know all these kids or are you just waving to strangers?' I asked.

'They're all my friends!'

'Then why don't you go play with them?'

'Because I want to be with you.'

He looked at me with such innocence, love and excitement that my stomach flipped. He only let go off my hand when the DJ started playing music and all the children took over the stage to showcase their lack of skills. Even there, my son's lack of talent shone through. And Rajiv must've read my expression because he said, 'So nice that he's enjoying himself.'

But I was worried. Where did his talent lie? Academically, he was pretty average. Musically, he had failed more than I cared to keep count. We'd pushed him to play sport—he'd been going for football since he was five, but he still ran away from the ball as if it would sting him rather than connecting with it. And now he claimed an undying love for astronomy but knew nothing.

'What's Milky Way?' I quizzed him.

'Chocolate?'

'It's a galaxy.'

'That's also chocolate.'

And when I thought about it, there are way too many chocolates named after celestial bodies, so I wrote to some of my friends in the industry and told them how terribly unethical it was to keep such brand names. But they all sent me LOL sort of messages. I hated people who said 'LOL'.

'Can I go to Aryan's house tomorrow?' Kevin asked me as we sat down with a plate of very oily food after all the games and dancing. 'For Diwali?'

'No, we'll have a quiet family thing at home,' I told him.

'You won't be working?' He sounded surprised.

'I never work on Diwali!'

'You worked last year.'

'That was an aberration.'

'Will there be an abortion this year too?'

'Aberration you mean and no.'

He looked at me delighted and returned to his plate of bhaturas.

'Hey, Leela! Hey, Mira!' he shouted out to more of his friends. 'Look, I'm here with my parents!'

'Kev, you must never speak with your mouth full!' I scolded him but then it suddenly struck me. What my mind map had been trying to tell me all this while. I quickly wiped my hands on my jeans and took out my phone.

'You said you won't be working!' Kevin moaned.

'Just five minutes, okay?' I promised as I emailed Silky.

'Gis, I think you should stick to your word,' Rajiv warned.

'But I just need to send this one email.'

'Gis ...' I looked up at Rajiv who was watching me meaningfully. I sighed and put my phone away. Fine. It was Diwali anyway. I tore a piece of bhatura and dipped it in oil-soaked channa. Yum.

Pareeta

Week 36

'Pareeta Di, you've outdone yourself.'
I smiled at my cousin sister as she reached into a box of laddus. Mama loved having the family over the day before Diwali, and the house was brimming with her siblings, my siblings, cousins, spouses and millions of children. My sister came loaded with flowers and candles to do up the house, and I, as always, came bearing deep fried snacks and six varieties of sweets.

The excitement of this annual meet was unmatched. I knew diaries had been blocked and outfits had been purchased weeks in advance. Mama had worked tirelessly over the menu, Papa had stocked up his bar, one of my niece was now grown up enough to take over the music and now, Mama was seated ensconced between her three sisters and two sisters-in-law, all of them beaming in each other's company, engaging in a match of who could outshout the other.

I had already accepted all the congratulations that had poured my way with hugs and kisses and compliments of how I was glowing and now sat with my swollen feet up on the pouf. Of course, Pankaj was missing it. Second year in a row.

'I need to close this now, Pareeta, otherwise I'll have to spend another month stuck here,' he'd said.

Just thinking of him made me sad. He hadn't come for my birthday, he hadn't been able to video call on Karwa Chauth and I didn't even remember which country he was in currently. I fought back tears watching all the happy families around me pose for pictures, the cousins with their spouses, the younger ones with their partners and I rubbed my belly trying to find comfort in the baby. Surely it would change things? I felt a shiver of panic mixed with a wave of sadness. That's when I saw Vidya watching me from the corner of the room, so I quickly hid my pain behind a sunny smile. She knew something was amiss because she walked across the room, balancing on her high heels, her tall glass of aam panna in her hand, looking absolutely stunning in her orange lehenga, her hair straightened and with silver jhumkis in her ears. How quickly they grow up! How proud you feel of them! I had sent Pankaj a picture of both kids this evening—Vidya smiling beautifully, Aryan with his big, gap-toothed grin—but hadn't received a response. Of course, Kevin had walked in and looked shocked that we were headed to a party without him, so we pulled him in for a family photograph as well. A family photograph—without Pankaj.

'Are you okay, Mom?' Vidya asked sitting down beside me.

'Absolutely fine, baby,' I said rubbing her knee.

'You look uncomfortable. Are you in labour?'

'No. It's not time yet.'

'Anuja Didi was shocked to see you today. Nobody had told her and she said she met you last month.'

'All the rolls of fat helped keep it a secret, I guess?' I laughed and she smiled.

'Seriously though. Are you okay? You look pale. Should I call Nani?'

'Oh no, absolutely not! Are you having fun?'

'Yes, I am. Kriti got me a really nice nail paint. See?'

I studied her neon-green nails staying as poker-faced as I could but then she caught me and rolled her eyes.

'You hate it.'

'I don't love it,' I said honestly.

She shook her head and looked around. 'I love Nani's Diwali party. It's so much fun being part of a big family.'

I wondered whether she meant it, given that we were indeed going to be a big family ourselves.

'Imagine there will be four of us next year!' she exclaimed.

My heart lurched as I realized she wasn't counting Pankaj. Then I realized that she could have missed the baby. She hadn't taken one of them into account and I worried which one she'd left out. Before I could ask, Aryan came running with a cousin of his and placed a hand on my stomach.

'There! That's my little brother.'

'Inside that?' a stunned-looking Ashwin asked. 'Why did Pareeta Maasi *eat* it?'

'No, silly! She's growing it inside her ... Like the science lab.'

'What's a lab?'

Aryan tutted. 'Oh, I forgot! You're only in Grade I. In Grade III, you start going to the lab.'

'Why doesn't my Mama go to the lab?' Ashwin whined. 'I also want a brother!'

'What makes you think it's a brother and not a sister?' Vidya asked snarkily.

'Because if there are any more girls in the house, I'll go mad!' Aryan said dramatically.

'What does that mean?' I asked in amusement.

'You, Didi, Nirmala Didi, Amla Didi, Urmi Didi. There are too many girls!'

'If it's a girl,' Ashwin negotiated, 'can you give it to Mama, Pareeta Maasi? I want a sister.'

Aryan raised his nose. 'Miss Ambika said only the most special people have brothers and sisters. I told her I already had one, of course, but she said that I must be super special to have two. Now I can be both big brother *and* small brother.'

I didn't know when Miss Ambika had had that conversation with him and I was a bit taken aback.

'When did she tell you that?'

'When I found out you weren't telling me.'

'You knew I wasn't telling you?'

Aryan averted his eyes sheepishly. 'Well, I was a bit angry earlier because I kept hearing the word "baby" at home so when I told her there was a baby coming and I didn't want it, she told me I was lucky because, do you know she also has a big brother? And she said big brothers are like Batman, they look after you. Can you imagine? I'm going to be Batman!' He grinned gleefully.

Vidya ruffled his hair. 'Aw, my little imp. You're already my little Joker!'

'Vidya!' I warned.

The boys scuttled off to watch Nanu's new television and Vidya stood up to join her cousins. Then, she paused and looked at me seriously.

'Mom, if there's anything bothering you, you can tell me, okay? I'm not a child any more.' My eyes stung but I smiled and waved her to go. I sat back and thought of what Aryan had said. I didn't know when Miss Ambika had had that conversation with him but it had helped, obviously. I guess I should thank her in a way.

Suddenly her words rang true. *Are you saving your marriage?*

It was *that* obvious, even to a stranger. This baby was to save my marriage.

I picked up my phone, walked to the balcony and dialled Pankaj. It began ringing and I didn't even bother calculating the time difference. It went into voicemail so I called again. And again. And again. My fingers were shaking as I tried him a fourth time, wondering what if I had been in labour.

Then I received a text.

> Can't talk right now. In a meeting. Please leave a message.

I looked at my phone for a long time and then finally keyed it out.

> We need to talk.

Sometimes you don't realize what's going on in your own life till someone holds up a mirror for you.

Riddhi

Weight: No battery in machine. Had to take it out when it read 74 kgs
Diet Plan: Bhaad mein gayi

I was toh so sad, *so* sad don't even ask. Not because weighing machine stopped working but because when we sat in the car after Miss Ambika's stupid apology, Jia told me why she wore so much make-up. Because she had scar on face because her ganda sa, ghatiya sa husband had beaten her up. It made me even sadder because I always thought Jia was so strong—she left husband because he was cheating or something. But beating up was too much. My Harsh would never do anything like that. Even when we fought, I would tell him things and he would just say, Arrey yaar, Riddhi. And then nothing.

I couldn't believe I was not so appreciating Harsh. He only wanted my goodness by making me want to thin down. When had I become such an unappreciating person? First, I don't appreciate husband. And now teacher says I don't appreciate daughter.

I was toh so sad, I didn't even go for party which was one plus one party! Pre-Diwali as well as Vikas Bhaiya's fortieth birthday. But I decided no more self-obsession. I had to be with my children. So I sat with Shivam and read him a story—though only I was reading to all bhoot-pret because he didn't listen to anything, and kept running round and round in circles. Then I came to Syra's room and she was reading some book, and was so shocked to see me. I didn't have much to talk about to her but I let her read and then thought I'd pat her to sleep.

'Kyun re, Riddhi? Why Why aren't you coming?'

I cradled the phone under my chin and kept patting. 'Yaar, Delhi side is difficult to come.'

'Vikas ki fortieth hai, yaar.'

'Weekend pe karenge na celebrate after Diwali.'

'Saari party everyone will ask about you only.'

It was true. What's a party without Riddhi Makheeja Chhabra? I patted Syra even harder.

'Ow!' she cried.

'Kya?' I asked her and then turned back to the phone. 'Chal, Mamta. I'll call you tomorrow, okay? Keep posting photos on WhatsApp and Insta. Make reel also, okay? Proper with ... *Zara zara* song.' I almost choked because I really wanted to be at that party and had Dolly Aunty make me a black sequin saree because theme was Black Label, but now my mood was so sado, so sado, I couldn't change out of my night suit only. Was Miss Ambika right? Did I dress too OTT? But why shouldn't I? What was life without colour? Even if it was black colour.

'This is so weird!'

I looked down at Syra and she was looking at me with one eye, like Lalita Pawar.

'What's weird?'

'This. You trying to put me to bed. You've never done this before.'

'I do it every night!'

'To Shivam, not to me.'

Uff! Try to be nice to this one and this is what you hear! Miss Ambika should try this once. Give same level of love to both children and one doesn't appreciate only.

'Why you not sleeping?' I asked her.

'Why do you look so worried?'

I groaned. 'Don't try to be amma, now, Syra. Close your eyes and sleep!'

'If you stop banging your hands on me, I will.'

I pushed her away and she giggled. 'Chal, so jaa!' I bent down, she gave me a hug and I kissed her forehead.

Back in my room, Shivam was sprawled across my bed, his NERF gun still in his hand. I took the gun away and went to lie down next to him. I gave him a hug and he kicked me in my stomach. Maybe Miss Ambika was right. I was wasting all my love on the wrong child.

Harsh walked into the room wearing parrot-green suit and his pant so high you could see his Versace socks.

'Sure you don't want to come?' he asked again spraying himself with so much perfume whole Mall of Dubai could have fainted.

I became ball. Matlab not round like a ball weight-wise but I pulled knees to chin and became like a ball. He looked at me all worried.

'Has Shivam done something? Do we need another driver?' Harsh tried to guess.

'Uff! Har baar same emergency! And there is no emergency, I already told you. Vaise why are you wearing green? Theme is black.'

'I have to go to Golf Club first. I told Kishore to keep my black suit in the car. But first to the club party. It'll be good for networking.'

Someone should put Jio booster box on my Harsh—all network issues will be solved for entire city. So much he was roaming around.

'What happened? What siyappa have you done now?' he asked.

I got so angry I became aag baboola …. What's it called in English? I became fume. Why did Harsh think I only do siyappa!

'What all siyappa have I done that you think I only do? Why you think your wife only is always wrong?'

He became gentler and sat next to me. I pushed him away and pulled my purple silk dressing gown from under him.

'Are you still thinking about the stupid note?'

Tears welled up in my eyes.

'Har cheez mein my fault. Shivam threw Alexa on driver, my fault.'

'When did he throw Alexa?'

'When it kept giving Wikipedia definition of kaccha badaam instead of playing the song.'

'But on the driver!'

'Driver was standing outside. What can I do?'

'We need to take him to a counsellor, Riddhi. His temper tantrums are too much.'

'I told him the same thing. You have too much tantrums, Bhaiyaji. Baccha hai.'

'I meant Shivam. He needs counselling.'

I lost it! 'Tumhara bas chaley toh everyone should go to counsellor. Shivam for anger, Syra for high IQ and me for my psycho obsession with food. We are Punjabi, Harsh! We like our food! You do too much diet-diet, exercise-exercise, Harsh. It's Diwali week and I'm eating banana before going for dinners, having beetroot juice instead of cocktails, eating dates instead of dessert.'

God knows why I was discussing food—maybe it was because I saw a reel on how people of Gujarat are making chocolate ice cream idli vada and it made me want to cry.

'Riddhi,' he said softly holding my hand, 'I'm sorry. I'm sorry for putting pressure on you.'

'I'm only 69 kgs, Harsh,' I argued weakly. Maybe argued is not right term. Lied is more accurate. 'There are bigger women than me also! Vikas ki biwi, Ajit ki biwi, Tannu, Kitty, Madhuri—'

'Arrey yaar, it's not about them. And it's not about fat either.'

'So then what?' I was crying now, stupid damn tears spoiling carefully put expensive night cream. 'Am I not pretty anymore? I know thhoda I do have stomach, but—'

'You're so beautiful, Riddhi, what are you saying! You're Riddhi Makheeja! You're *my* Riddhi Makheeja. RMC! My heart still beats so much when I see you get ready for party. Rajouri ke boys will cut off their wrist for you even now!'

That made me feel a bit happy and I wiped my tears. Not like I wanted people to cut their vein for me but it was good to know that I could still ask them to. For blood donation and all, I mean. I am very kind-hearted.

Harsh looked down at his hands guiltily. 'The truth is, Riddhi, this all has to do with Mummy's death. Mummy was everything, you know that.'

I knew how much Harsh was upset when Mummyji died. One sudden heart attack after a chaat party at Khosla Aunty's house and we thought so again she has indigestion. But she was gone. Harsh had gone into shock. He's youngest in family—except one brother who is younger and also one sister who is younger—and he was very close to Mummyji. So was I. In fact, she was the one who introduced me to Dolly Aunty, my boutique lady.

A mother-son bond is very different. Mother-daughter bond is also different but mother-daughter also fight. With sons, they think you're centre of their universe. They need their Mamas like they need oxygen.

'If Mummyji had looked after her health, she would have been okay,' Harsh was saying. 'She would have lived longer. Papa ki bua is still alive! She's ninety-two and she's so active that she knows what's cooking in everyone's kitchen in the colony!'

I shuddered at her name because she's the one who had told the family that Harsh and I were having affair. 'But because Buaji takes care of her health, she lived on. Lekin Mummy just ate too much deep fried and jalebi and did this to her heart.'

'Main bhi toh take care karti hoon, Harsh. I go to the gym!' Because there's no place one can socialize more than at the gym. You discuss gym clothes and compare calories burnt on your Apple watch, and then go for coffee and cake with friends.

He looked like he wanted to say something but didn't. He just squeezed my hand. 'I didn't say anything because of your looks. I only care for your health. Tujhe kuch ho gaya toh?'

It sounds very filmy but he said it with lot of emotion, so I felt very moved and my eyes also started watering again. I cried into his shoulder and he cried into mine—big baby he is—and I realized how much I loved him. I'll start proper diet from tomorrow only. Or maybe Monday. Or post Diwali hols.

'And don't get worried about stupid teacher note, yaar, Riddhi.'

Pata nahin what happened to him, I think so finally Harsh has become old and mature or something because he said, 'Sach hi toh likha hai. Jia does wear too much make-up, Giselle ko phone se fursat nahin, you only say Pareeta's husband is never around and teri Goa-wali friend ... Who wouldn't prefer Goa to Delhi? Main bhi soch raha hoon, we should start business unit in Goa.'

'But what about what she wrote about me?' I asked even though I wanted to discuss Goa business because hai, I could show off how we travelled to Goa for every holiday. But we could discuss that later.

'How does it matter, yaar? It's her personal document. I also bitch about clients, no? Saala Raja who keeps seeing houses only and has no money to buy anything. Or that Mr Arora who wants better investment, better investment, but even best investment he doesn't like. Or Mr Handa who buys just when the bid is closed. Or Mrs Sen who keeps doing vaastu rejection of all property and Mrs Tuli who keeps saying, "Feel nahin aa rahi". Everyone cribs, yaar. The women in your kitty must be talking worse about you when you don't attend.'

Which was true. That's why I never missed a single kitty.

'And as long as Syra likes her—for the first time I think she likes a teacher—then it's fine, no? Tu dil pe mat le, yaar.'

Kainaz

	Either:
1.	She was sick: Not terminally sick or anything, but just sick with lots of viruses and other germs hovering around her, ready to latch on to the lesser mortals she'd invited to her house.
2.	She was angry: She'd called it an 'emergency meeting'. Honestly, I had felt a bit angry at being at her beck and call too; maybe she was really going to lash out at us.

Irrespective, here I was, two days after Diwali, sitting in a house that I would totally not associate with someone like Giselle Savarkar. I expected it to be more lavish, expensive, meticulous—much like how she looked. But it was untidy, mismatched, bulky and really quite hideous. Perhaps it reflected the state of her mind.

Riddhi looked positively delighted to be invited and couldn't stop gaping at everything.

'It's been five years since I've known her, Kainazji, but never been invited. Maybe we're friends?' she asked gleefully. Though it looked like she too hoped that the house had more to offer. It was the same layout as Pareeta's, very spacious with large balconies and bright interiors but it lacked finesse. What a waste of beautiful space! It almost looked like the Museum of Illusions Ahaan and I had visited with some things too big for the room, some too small.

Jia looked sullen to have had to drop work to be here. She looked tired and could do with a glass of water but none was offered to us.

'I have to be at office by eleven,' Jia said but the comment was directed at the wrong people. It should have been at the host, who looked in no tearing hurry to tell us why we were here, and just seated herself in a large armchair and checked her email. We waited patiently for Pareeta, sitting in awkward silence, and I wondered if this was just a build up to tell us that she'd already taken action against Miss Ambika and done her most favourite thing in the world—sent an email? Or perhaps this was just her invitation for tea?

We all sat twiddling our thumbs as Pareeta texted that she would take another ten minutes as she was finishing an order. Riddhi leaned in and whispered, 'I have an in-laws-side kitty at twelve. If I reach late, that Maya will start tambola without me and, not like I'm interested in prizes—it's always some glass set with that side, very cheap—but without me, nobody knows the variation. They'll just do corners, top row, bottom row and it'll all be so boring. Have you done saas-bahu variation?'

My expression must've given it away because she nodded smugly. 'See? So many I know. No party is complete without me. Very pheeka. I hope Pareetaji turns up quickly.'

Then she immediately turned to Jia.

'Your cheque has come? What do you plan to do? Go on a trip with Rabia! That would be my suggestion. We're booked for Milan in June. But I did lots of research on other locations also. Like Dharamshala. I'll share. Our travel agent gives very good discount. His sister and I went to same tuition centre for plus two. Papaji insisted I do mathematics. Kya bheja kharaab hua hai!'

Jia just smiled, so Riddhi mustered up the courage to turn to her third target.

'Giselleji, don't you have office today? I think so no more holidays now even though—'

'I've taken the week off.'

I could see the flash of panic in everyone's eyes. Riddhi grabbed my hand and said in a hushed voice, 'Has she called us because she's going on holiday and wants us to watch Kevin? Nahin, yaar, nahin. We're not *that* good friends also!'

Pareeta breezed in then, looking very flushed and tired.

'Sorry I'm so late.'

We exchanged pleasantries and Giselle rapped the armchair to call the meeting to a start.

'So,' she said authoritatively, 'what have we decided about Ambika?'

There was silence. I knew the silence meant nobody knew the right answer. The right answer was whatever Giselle wanted. She looked around the room and we all stayed mum. Then, perhaps because I was least scared of her, I spoke up. And also because I knew Ambika best.

'I am personally willing to forgive Miss Ambika for what has happened,' I started. 'It wasn't a nice thing for her to say, but I understand why she said it. And I think everything she's done for Ahaan to help him settle in outweighs what she said about me. Honestly, maybe she was just having a bad day.'

'Bad day ka toh pata nahin,' Riddhi said, 'but Harsh says it was her personal point of view and we shouldn't have read it. Matlab, I can read it but not react to it. People in kitties talk like this all the time. Once a month, we even do lady by lady roasting. It's anonymous, of course. I couldn't tell Kamini on her face that her cleavage display is too much.'

'What's wrong with showing a little bit of cleavage?' Giselle flared up. 'We're women. It's a part of our body. I'm tired of being apologetic for who I am!'

'Uff, Giselleji, you think I'm too backward!' She pulled out her phone and scrolled down. Then she held up a picture that made all of us gasp. Even Giselle blinked a few times too many.

'I agree,' Pareeta added. 'I think I got offended because she told the truth. About Pankaj being an absent parent and me having this baby to save my marriage.' She looked down at her hands and I felt a bit embarrassed. 'It is, after all, her personal opinion. We weren't meant to see it. Riddhi's husband is right. Maybe because she's a teacher, we expect her not to be judgmental, whereas so many people we come across may feel and say worse things about us. I'm so glad we heard her out, took a break because it certainly helped me think clearly.'

'But that's just the point. She's a *teacher*,' Giselle pointed out. 'She's in a position of authority. She isn't allowed to make such slips.'

'I think the thing is,' Pareeta said, 'Kainaz, Riddhi and I feel she told the truth about us—maybe it wasn't needed or maybe it was—but she's been kind to our children and we don't want to lodge a complaint. What about you, Jia? What about you, Giselle?'

Without waiting for Jia's response, Giselle stood up and we witnessed some courtroom drama. And delightfully, a list.

1.	As a teacher, she was a figure of authority. She had exploited that power.
2.	Children were impressionable. If she carried angst about us, it would percolate down to them.
3.	The judgement was simply unfair. We have our own set of challenges and are working to the best of our capabilities, but nobody seemed to hear us out. And women against women was simply unacceptable.
4.	We're already dealing with guilt about our choices every day and trying hard to do the balancing act, and this is an outright insult of our efforts.

Just when I thought she was on the other side of the camp, and felt myself veering to that side too, she switched.

'But she held up a light to us. We owned up to our misgivings—not in terms of parenting but judging each other. We learnt to be more sensitive towards each other. We learnt tolerance, acceptance and we became friends. So maybe we should give her another chance.'

Everyone nodded in agreement and it felt like a weight had been lifted off everyone's shoulders in the room. We all felt more relaxed. More like ourselves. Pareeta was the first one to voice how glad she was to get this episode over and done with. Riddhi said we should all celebrate a better phase of womanhood and started to plan a party. Jia volunteered to send an email to Miss Ambika on our behalf letting her know of our decision. Giselle, for the first time, smiled and offered to bring out something to eat now that we were all gathered anyway.

Just as I was taking a bite of the biscotti from the plate, Giselle sat down next to me, while the others chatted, and looked me straight in the eye.

'So, how much do you know?'

I looked at her and there was a knowing look in her eye. I knew she knew. My heart start racing.

'Actually it was only recently that—'

'So you do know.'

'Yes but—'

'And it has no bearing on your decision.'

'Ladies,' Jia said suddenly. 'There's an email.'

Lesson Thirteen
Accounting

From: The Desk of the Principal, CVS
To: happyriddhi@tmail.com, Giselle.savarkar@hirearchy.com, Jia@avstech.com, pareetaspastries@tmail.com, kainaz.dotwalla@tmail.com
Date: 10 November 2022 at 2:55 PM
Sub: Meeting

Dear Parents,

I am extremely sorry for my absence and not being able to resolve your issues. I have received your email and I understand it requires my immediate intervention. I would therefore like to invite you for a quick discussion tomorrow at 11 a.m. as we hold a disciplinary meeting against Miss Ambika S.

Regards,

Malini Mehta
Principal, Champion Valley School

Riddhi

Weight: No machine. No weight.
Diet Plan: Bran roti, which I misread as 'brain' roti, so I got Gullu ka bheja fry and ate with roomali roti

Pehle toh I read it wrong. I thought what dispensary meeting is this? Are we on some nurse room committee? Then I realized it's disciplinary. Means, Mrs Mehta was suspending Miss Ambika.

Everyone had read the email in confusion again. Giselleji's email had only said we wanted to meet her. How she knew we wanted to complain about Miss Ambika? Then we all understood—one of us had sent an email about it without telling others.

It was like suspense movie!

I would think it would have been Giselle Savarkar only because she toh loved writing emails to complain. But she looked as surprised as us.

Maybe it was Jia. She was only one who hadn't said much about note. I looked over at her. But no, no, I could not doubt my bestie.

Maybe it was Kainaz. Maybe bhaisaheb—matlab handsome hunk Varaz—had an affair with Miss Ambika and that's how they knew each other. Now Kainaz was seeking revenge.

Maybe it was Pareeta. Maybe her pregnancy hormones made her brain go crazy.

I felt like I was also going crazy. My toh head swam like Kareena in *Talaash* last lake scene.

By god, like Harsh liked to say, Miss Ambika would now face the music. Or like we say in Rajouri, uska toh band baj gaya.

I went home and showed email to Harsh. He was so surprised he turned as red as his F1 jacket. Why he wore that I didn't know. Maybe he was selling venue for Grand Pricks.

'You have to come also,' I told him.

'Why? Now that the meeting is happening, tell Mrs Mehta what happened.'

'But I don't want Miss Ambika to get into trouble any more. I feel bad for her. I think so she is gareeb.'

'So is Lalita Didi, but you don't feel bad for her.'

'That's not fair. I just did Lalita's life insurance and medical insurance.'

'Because of the "buy two get one" scheme and the drivers insisted we get them insured given Shivam's behaviour.' He started to laugh. 'Arrey yaar, Riddhi, I'm joking only. Fine, I'll come. When?'

'Tomorrow.'

'But I have a meeting with Mr Bajaj.'

I gave him one of my looks. He immediately came on track. 'I'll postpone it.'

'Better. And not that I'm paying attention to Miss Ambika's note but dress properly. Not this jacket-shacket.'
'It's a Gautam Gupta.'
'Toh usko vapis kar do. Borrow kiya hi kyun?'

Kainaz

'God, nothing half as exciting ever happened in Goa,' Varaz had said when he'd read the disciplinary mail last evening.

'I wouldn't use the term exciting.'

'It's insane ... I feel for her.'

'You would. She's your ex.'

'She's not my ex.'

'You slept with her.'

'And didn't even remember her. So which one of the mums did it?'

I looked at him and shrugged.

He raised an eyebrow. 'What does that mean? Did you ...?'

———•———

'Inko dekha hai? Looking like a peacock!' Riddhi hissed pointing towards her husband who was busy in a conversation with Giselle's husband. We were sitting around the conference room waiting for Mrs Mehta to make an appearance.

'Such a bright blue suit ki I had to wear my sunglasses only! And that gold chain hanging from his pocket? Miss Ambika says I look like fairy tale? Look at him. Looking like Prince Charlie!'

'Prince Charles,' I corrected her.

She ignored me and brushed invisible specks of dust off her own saree. 'I mean, I had to wear dull grey saree to balance off the amount of colour he's wearing.'

I didn't want to point out that her dull grey saree had glittering pink flowers and gold embroidery, plus her golden hair clip against her golden bleached hair made her look much shinier than her husband—instead, I just smiled. That was just so Riddhi. So unbridled.

Harsh suddenly leaned forward and raised his eyebrows. 'Kya? Again about my gold chain?'

'It looks cheap, Harsh!' she scowled.

'I have to meet a client after this,' he explained to us, 'who deals with watches.' He pulled out a pocket watch attached to the gold string. 'This will impress him, nahin?'

I was dumbfounded and so was Varaz. Sometimes, Varaz agreed with me that indeed, the city was a bit weird. It never ceased to surprise you—in Riddhi's case, shock you. I bit back the urge to laugh.

We all heard some commotion in the hallway outside and in walked Mrs Mehta, followed by two other staff members. One I recognized as Miss Shilpa Anand, the grade coordinator, who looked hugely troubled by the turn of events. The other one seemed to be an assistant of sorts. Trudging in right behind them was a very dejected-looking Ambika, who refused to meet anyone's eye. She looked very unlike herself. Younger somehow. More sulky, less in control, more exasperated. Or maybe it was just my imagination.

'I apologize for having disrupted your schedules at such short notice,' Mrs Mehta began, her voice very nasal, still recovering from the illness that had kept her out of action for the last few days. 'I hope you're all comfortable and have been given some tea?'

'Haanji, sugar was a little bit less though,' Riddhi complained and I could see Harsh kick her under the table.

'Sorry about that.' Mrs Mehta looked at the assistant who immediately sprung up from his seat and called one of the office boys to bring a pot of sugar. There was barely any tea left so another kettle was brought in, and only when Riddhi tasted it and was satisfied did the meeting commence.

'Without taking too much time, we're here to discuss the very unfortunate and rather irresponsible event that took place a month ago.'

'Wait, aren't we going to wait for the other two?' Giselle interrupted.

'Mrs Mazumdar, Rabia's mother, has sent her regrets that she will not be able to join us as she has a work commitment. And Mrs Singh, Aryan's mother, hasn't been answering the phone.'

I looked over at Giselle and she at me. Being absent was telling. Had one of them sent out the email and couldn't face us now?

Mrs Mehta knotted her heavily solitaired fingers on the table, a whiff of Elizabeth Arden traversing the room. She studied each of the us individually with watchful, hawk-like eyes.

'As you know, we've received a complaint.'

Giselle

Time: 11.05 a.m.
Unread emails (4,100)

I cleared my throat. 'Mrs Mehta, we had only requested for a meeting. We hadn't filed a complaint.'

'Yes, but the meeting was to file a complaint, was it not?'

'Yes,' she agreed, 'but the meeting was ...'

'What do you mean?'

FFS! 'We don't want to pursue the complaint. We requested for a meeting, which, thank you for granting, but the matter has been mutually resolved and we don't need to talk about it now.'

I shot Kainaz and Riddhi a look. They took the hint, and immediately sprung to action and nodded in agreement. Ambika looked at us in shock.

'And why, may I ask, have you decided to drop the complaint?' Mrs Mehta asked, casting a rather stern look at Ambika.

'We understand it was a mistake,' Kainaz spoke up.

'Yes,' Riddhi added excitedly. 'Even at my kitty, too much bitching happens. But Miss Ambika, she's okay. Our children like her. We've forgiven her.'

Mrs Mehta was silent for a minute and the other two people in the team exchanged a confused look.

'That is very kind of you all,' the principal began holding up a paper, 'thank you for being so generous. But the fact remains that we do have this note and it goes completely against the ethos of what our school stands for.'

So it was the note in question. Someone had not only asked for this meeting but also shared the parent's report card with her. There were murmurs around the room and Rajiv was saying something but I interrupted him. One of us had to be direct.

'Sorry, Mrs Mehta, but how did that note even reach you?'

'What?'

'That note. Who sent it?'

Ambika was frowning too, sitting up straighter. Suddenly Jia burst into the room.

'I'm so sorry I'm late!' She turned to Mrs Mehta and beamed at her. 'Good morning, Mrs Mehta. So sorry. I've had a crazy morning.'

I couldn't help but notice how pleased she sounded. She turned to us and I felt a jolt of shock. She looked so different. Not a spot of make-up. Her features looked so much sharper, her skin so buttery, the scar—an angry red gash—sat on her cheek but did nothing to mar her beauty. And her eyes, so bright, so excited. She walked up to an empty seat behind Varaz, stopping only briefly to squeeze Ambika's shoulder on the way and to hold Riddhi's hand. She even looked at me and smiled.

Jia Mazumdar! Smiled!

Mrs Mehta cleared her throat. 'As I was telling Mrs Savarkar here, Ms Mazumdar, we received a letter of complaint along with a scan of this "report card" titled the "Fabulous Lives of Mums".

'Yes,' Jia said sitting down. 'But which one of us sent it?'

Ambika

It was only November. Some argue it's the best month of the year in Delhi. But I'd felt a terrible chill when I'd walked into her office yesterday and had to sit on my hands to keep my fingertips from freezing. My teeth had been chattering and the smell of her Elizabeth Arden had made me sick.

'A bad day? *A bad day*? You wrote this note because you were having a bad day? What do you think will happen if, I don't know, Kim Jong-Un has a bad day?'

'I guess he'd bomb America?'

'No. He would destroy millions of innocent lives. Which is what you've done with your *bad day*!'

I didn't like being called Kim Jong-Un. I could barely manage a dictation test without giving hints to my students, let alone be a dictator of a country. I wanted to crack that joke but it wasn't the time for that and Mrs Mehta was not the sort of person you could crack jokes with. Dodo would appreciate it, though, if I survived to tell the tale.

'I can't believe … I can't believe you've done this! I *gave* you this job! I trusted you, I've spent so much time and effort ensuring our standards were not being compromised by hiring an untrained teacher! And then you go ahead and do *this*?'

Fuck. This was bad. Very, very bad. I cleared my throat. 'I'm really so sorry, Mrs Mehta. I don't know who sent you the email but I'd already settled it with the mums. I'd admitted my mistake, apologized and—'

'Ambika, apologizing doesn't help!'

God, she was so angry she hadn't even called me *Am*bika. She actually stood up and started pacing the room. I felt even more sick. Suddenly, I thought of Kevin, who often admitted to having 'emotion sickness' on long car journeys. That's how I was feeling.

Damn. I'd miss being his teacher. There were so many such gems that these kids threw at you every day that, even on the worst of days, made you laugh. But I couldn't at this time. It would be severe breach of discipline as per the 'Discipline for Teachers' training module.

'Your actions are a reflection of *our* school, they impact the perception of *our* school. And in a school as well regarded as ours, there is so much *more* at stake. My PR and communication team is just going to …' She just stopped talking and held her forehead, like she couldn't bear it, looking out of the window, shaking her head. 'I'm sorry, but I have to take disciplinary action against you. Otherwise no child, no parent, nobody will ever feel safe here!'

God, she was so dramatic. I wasn't a serial killer. 'Can't we just say I didn't do it? That one of my students copied my handwriting?'

'But did they, Miss Ambika? *Did they?*' she snapped and I shrunk in my seat.

The last time she'd been this angry was when we were back in school, and her beloved son had crawled into the girls hostel to deliver a love note and had been caught by the warden. It had been a scary sight because we all thought that by then we knew what an angry Mrs Mehta looked like but had no idea how much angrier and scarier she could actually get.

I cleared my throat. 'Mrs Mehta, don't you think something similar would happen if CCTV footage of the staff room was ever released? In fact, the remarks that fly there are far more insinuating than the innocent ...' I noticed her glare and retracted quickly, 'harmless ... I mean, you know, than my note.'

'If that were to happen,' she replied sharply, 'it would give Champion Valley School a very bad name. But I trust my teachers and know we treat every child, every parent with respect like they're a part of our family. And *we* don't insult our family! I don't know what happens in *your* family, Miss *Ambika* but in *our* family, in *our* Champion Valley family, we only help hold up the honour and trust of our students, our parents and our staff!'

Shit. I was in big trouble.

'Mrs Mehta,' I implored, 'I know in an ideal world it shouldn't happen at all. But it does happen in the staff rooms. I'm sure it does. I don't even spend so much time in the staff room myself but—'

'Well, I do and this kind of conversation never takes place!'

She would be surprised by how often she's the subject of some of these conversations but I bit my tongue instead.

'These mums have raised a complaint,' Mrs Mehta said catching her breath and sitting down in resignation. 'And that's the reality of it! As a school, we have to act upon it, show accountability. *Your* actions are *our* responsibility.'

She gave me one of her icy dagger looks and, as always, it silenced me. Her phone buzzed and I looked out of the cabin as she answered. Shilpa Anand was hovering around the admin area on a bloody Sunday. Which was just strange. Did she really work all weekends? Of course, the admin team was there too, but they literally lived on the premises and there was no way that Mrs Mehta was coming to school and they weren't. But Shilpa Anand ...

Well, that was yesterday. Today, Mrs Mehta was court-martialling me and throwing me to the lions. Defending the honour of the school and all. How did people fight cases for years and years? Twenty minutes into it and I was so bored, I just wanted them to pass the judgement and be done with it. So, okay, I was going to lose this job. And my dignity. But I'd find something else. I had experience now. Maybe nobody would want me as a teacher but I could be a secretary or something. I'd become pretty good with email writing, to start with. Or, I looked over at the assistant, who was taking notes silently and efficiently, I could do that. I could be a note-taker.

Mrs Mehta was now pacing the room, talking about the school and the pillars it was built on. One in particular: Consciousness. The word I still didn't understand. Bloody hell, it was coming to bite me in the ass now. I should've paid more attention.

'The fact that we know that a note had been written means we have to act upon it. Even if no complaint was registered,' Mrs Mehta was saying. I was all set to be marched off to the guillotine.

If I was honest, I was also pretty tired of myself. I was tired of screwing up things all the time. I thought, for once, whatever my motivation, I was doing a good job. I followed lesson plans to the T, improvised to make learning easier, could see the children being interested in what I was saying, learning concepts, becoming comfortable, I was being more patient, not calling them snotty monsters anymore and, if I was really, really, really being honest, then yes, I was also enjoying it a bit too—especially my time with Syra and Kevin. The age of eight was a good one, they were at the cusp of growing up.

Oh well, it had been a good stint. I'd felt responsible and committed, and, other than the last week of 'forced leave', I had actually walked into school every single day feeling pretty much in control. As much as one can be at the crack of dawn.

I let my mind drift once again to Dodo, who had insisted on coming with me today. I told him to shut it and stay at home so he'd done literally that. He's stayed over last night at *my* home and had given me an extra-long hug before I left. I'd allowed myself to relax in it briefly before shaking him off.

'Don't finish the ice-cream,' I'd warned him.

'We'll have it together once you're back.'

'If I'm back,' I had said ominously.

'Don't be dramatic, Mira.'

'You're the one being dramatic, staying overnight and all. Go get yourself a girlfriend!'

And he'd looked at me strangely. I was so done with his meaningful glances.

Back at the conference room, Mrs Mehta refused to disclose who had raised the complaint. But everyone who sat in the room right now—the mums and dads—they were all fighting *for* me. And that felt ... pretty good, actually. Of course, Mrs Mehta continued to speak about how the trust of the CVS family had been broken and all that!

I looked over at Varaz but he wasn't looking at me. Had he told everyone the truth and that's why they were defending me? Or had they genuinely forgiven me?

Suddenly, everyone fell silent. I looked around but nobody was looking at me. They had turned to the door. Mrs Mehta stood frozen to the spot and, before I could register who could possibly garner so much authority, in he walked—dressed in dark jeans and a formal white shirt. Both Shilpa Anand and the assistant stood up straight too. Then he met my eyes and I glared at him.

There he was. My fucking brother.

Lesson Fourteen
Current Affairs

Dear Mr Saraogi,

It is with great sadness that I bring to your notice the misconduct by one of your teachers. This note was recovered at her desk—a highly demeaning, insulting and appalling report card on the parents. Are these the values we're imparting at Champion Valley School? Are these the sort of people you're hiring? As a parent, do I feel safe around this teacher? As a student? As a staff member? Can I even entrust her with the care of small children?

This abovementioned note (enclosed herewith) was discovered weeks ago and no action has been taken yet. Since we live by the values of Integrity, Perseverance and Consciousness, I request you to bring justice to the school.

Kindly take appropriate action immediately against the teacher, Miss Ambika S., Grade III B.

Regards,
A CVS Loyalist

Jia

> Jia, I've called you six times. Where are you?

> Jia?

At school

All ok?

> Yes all ok

> Did you drop off the papers?

Yes

> All in order?

Yes

It's done

> Thank god. Thank god!

> Why didn't you come home?

> I'm at Mrs Mehta's meeting

> It's now?

> Yes

> When will you be back home?

> In a bit

> What's going on?

> Sahil is here

> Sahil?

> Sahil Saraogi

> Sahil Saraogi? Why?

> Are you ok?

> Did you speak to him?

> Jia?

Kainaz

I had no idea who he was. But everyone stood around almost reverentially around him. I turned to Varaz but he shrugged. He had no idea either. We'd all stood up automatically though, parroting Mrs Mehta and her team, and waited for an introduction. She and the young man had moved to the corner of the room and were now talking in low tones as we started conjecturing the identity of this person. Miss Ambika looked positively miffed. Who was it? Her boyfriend? Husband?

'Parents,' Mrs Mehta finally announced, 'I'd like you all to meet Mr Saraogi.'

Riddhi gasped audibly and grabbed her husband's arm. 'This is Krishna Saraogi? Founder of Champion Valley School? Wait, he's dead. This must be Anil Saraogi. MD. Oh my god! He looks so much younger in real life! He's almost seventy. I see him every year in the school magazine but looks so much younger, no? Harsh, say hello!'

Just as Harsh Chhabra was about to comply, Mrs Mehta continued, 'Mr Sahil Saraogi is currently the president of the board of Champion Valley School.'

'Oh, achha. Not even Anil Saraogi. The son. Makes sense now.'

Sahil Saraogi. Owner of the school. I looked at Varaz and he at me. Wait! That meant he was Miss Ambika's brother.

Riddhi gasped again behind me. I turned to her. Did she know too?

'Oh no!' she said. 'That means proper disciplinary meeting for Miss Ambika! Even president of board is here. They're going to rusticate her! Remember, Harsh, when Preeto was rusticated? So much drama had happened. But he was student. She is teacher!'

And she wasn't *just* a teacher. I turned to Varaz who was now frowning. He caught my eye and we both turned to look at Ambika. She had looked listless earlier but now looked like she was positively fuming. And Sahil Saraogi gave her a look that pierced through the room, a mixture of disappointment and smugness. I immediately cringed.

Giselle caught my eye then. She knew. That's what she had been trying to tell me at her house.

'Please be seated,' Mrs Mehta said, and we all sat down a little unsure as Sahil Saraogi walked to the front of the room and cleared his throat.

'I received a note this morning. An anonymous tip-off, really. It was delivered to my office, and I wanted to come and see this for myself. I didn't realize you'd all be here or that this meeting was in progress. I would like to personally apologize to each one of you for Miss Mirambika's misdemeanour.'

'Mirambika?' Riddhi said. 'Who's she? Are we in the wrong meeting?'

Sahil Saraogi paused to look at Mrs Mehta.

Mrs Mehta explained, 'Miss Ambika's full name is Mirambika Sara—'

'Why do *you* have to apologize?' Ambika spat suddenly, speaking for the first time that morning. 'It's a mistake *I* made and I've already apologized. I've apologized directly to the parents and they've categorically said they don't want to raise a formal complaint!'

'Mirambika,' Mr Saraogi said sternly, 'this is no longer just about you and them. It's about the reputation of our school.'

'I know that, and I had already reached out to them and offered my sincerest apologies, Sahil!'

'That's Mr Saraogi for you.'

'And that's Mirambika Saraogi for you. So cut it out!' Not only did Mrs Mehta gasp, but so did the other people in the room. The peon dropped the tray of tea he had just brought in, the assistant started to fan himself, Shilpa Anand looked like she'd been stabbed, Riddhi turned the colour of her saree, Harsh Chhabra's eyes popped out and Jia looked like she'd seen a ghost.

Ambika

I'm Mirambika Saraogi. And I own Champion Valley School.
Alright, that's not fully true. My family owns it. I'm only on the board of directors because of tax reasons or the law or something. But basically, I do own the school. Sort of. At least, as much as my fuck-all brother does.

It's not like my family owns only the school. We have a lot of businesses. Of course, we're not the Ambanis—we actually started as tradesmen in Kolkata—but now we have presence in multiple industries such as textiles, auto parts, machinery, and, some thirty years ago, Dada decided he wanted to 'give back' to society. And thus the seed of Champion Valley School was sown.

We had a pretty privileged childhood. Albeit a slightly lonely one. I was shipped off to Mussoorie to a private all-girls boarding school, while my brother moved to Gwalior to one of those established generation after generation paramparik ones. Here, we met people who were as entitled, privileged and impossible as us, and we grew up spoilt and worlds apart.

Neither of us looked forward to holidays because our parents were always so busy and, as it is with a growing business, we viewed all relatives with suspicion and resistance.

Materially, we had everything. We took international holidays, travelled by private planes, stayed only in the best hotels and splurged so much more than what most people could only hope to earn in a year. Mentally, though, we needed significant amounts of therapy that we never invested in.

In our growing up years, my brother was some sort of techie whiz-kid, aced his academics, studied computer science in Bangalore, took off to America and, like me, didn't really give a rat's ass about family or business. He enjoyed his marijuana and his raves, and never looked back.

I, on the other hand, was sick of my peer group by the time I was twenty and took up globe-trotting as a hobby. I had been visiting home once when my Dad had called me down for dinner only to discover I'd taken off for Bhutan. Once, he went to Moscow for a business trip and found me roaming the streets. But nothing beat the time they were watching the news of a major earthquake in Japan and there I was on TV telling the journalist that it was the most thrilling twenty seconds of my life. We were that disconnected as a family.

But I had no qualms of staying connected with the family money—that I spent with gay abandon. And nobody seemed to mind it. Till Mom passed away and Dad sort of snapped out of the 'commercialism' of our lives. He demanded we all return and stay together as a family. He said he'd had enough of us drifting around like logs of wood in a river and that we needed to tighten the familial bonds for the sake of our lost mother. Sahil cleaned up and returned. *I did nothing of the sort.*

For years, they tried to get me home for Diwali and birthdays, but I had places to be, things to see, money to spend. Then, when Sahil took over the business a couple of years ago, things took a turn for the worse. For me, I mean. Suddenly I was answerable to my own sibling? Did I know how much of the family finances I was draining? Did I know I couldn't just buy myself a jet ski just because I wanted to? Or a hill for that matter? I tried telling him that Kufri was very picturesque and I was just being really responsible by not bidding for it when it was being offered at throwaway prices, but he was constantly pulling me up for going astray. Unfortunately, Dad agreed. He seemed to agree with Sahil a lot of late. And that wasn't working out very well for me.

So a few months ago, they gave me the ultimatum. Join the business and contribute, or else. I chose 'or else'. I stormed out of their house, vowing not to take a penny from them any more. And, on day four of staying at the Taj Palace Hotel, Sahil called to tell me that it didn't really count as moving out if they were still paying for my five-star property staycation. Sahil may have been right for the first time in his life, so I decided to seek help. I called Dodo, the only friend I had bothered to stay in touch with over the years.

> 'You kept saying the real estate market in Gurgaon was a great investment opportunity,' I told him when he answered my call.
> 'It's three in the morning, Mira.'
> 'I know how to tell the time, Dodo. Did you make an investment or not?'
> 'What?'

'Did you or did you not buy a house in Gurgaon?'
'I didn't.'
Shit.
'It's more of a flat than a house.'
I breathed a sigh of relief. 'Can I have it?'
'What?'
'Can I have the flat?'
'Can you have my flat?'
'Yes. Why are you so slow?'
'How do I put it? No, Mira. You can't just have my flat. I know you're used to buying hills and planes and all that, but—'
'It was a jet ski not a jet plane. Besides, I don't want to have it have it. I just want it on rent.'
'You want to rent my house?'
'Your flat.'
'Why?'
'Because I've moved out of my house and have no place to stay.'
'What? You've moved out of the farm? When? Where are you?'
'Never mind. Yes or no?'
'Mira ...'
'Yes or no?'
'Listen, I'm coming back next week. Go home till then.'
'Yes or no?'
His voice became a little more gentle. 'Of course you can have it ... rent it. But let's discuss this, okay? Don't do anything hasty.'
'When have I ever done anything hasty?'

And I had then hastily disconnected before he could answer that question.

The next step was finding a job. That was extremely painful. All these jobs on the portals were just so blah. It didn't help that I had dropped out of college and had no educational qualifications, but the ones that demanded less also paid less.

Then Sahil had turned up with Dodo at the flat one day and I had almost slammed the door on his face. I was in no mood for reconciliation.

'I have a proposal for you.' Sahil had sauntered in.

'I'm not marrying him,' I declared pointing to Dodo.

Sahil also sighed the way Dodo did with me. 'I meant that I can help you find a job.'

'I'm not working with Saraogi Enterprises under you, I've already told you that.'

'Work at the school.'

I had glared at Dodo. 'Your suggestion?'

Dodo had thrown his arms up. 'Come on, Mira. I think it's a great option. You'll get a salary, you'll learn the business, there's Mrs Mehta.'

'Oh god!' I had moaned in my hands. 'Mrs Mehta will think I'm an A1 twat.'

'Nothing she doesn't know right now,' rude bloody Sahil said. 'Though, Dhruv, I do think it's not Mirambika's cup of tea to be working at all. I don't think she can do it.'

'Of course I can do it!' I snapped.

He threw me a challenge. 'Here's a deal then. You do this for one year and we'll get you back on the rolls of the business.'

'Fuck you, Sahil. You know I have as much right over the business as you do.'

'Yes, but you've never shown any interest.'

'And I never will.'

'And we'd like that to change. We'd like you to show more responsibility by—'

'Who is this fucking we?'

'Dad and I. Mira, you have to show some interest in our business. Dad's built it with all his hard work and your insistence to stay out of it is ridiculous. We can't keep paying you for nothing.' He inhaled sharply. 'Look, I've made mistakes as well, okay? But we need to clean our act now.'

'I'm not joining the business,' I'd declared firmly. As much as I didn't want my dad's hard work to go down the drain, I really had no interest in taking upon any responsibility.

'Mira,' Dodo had said patiently, 'listen to me. If you need to work, this is a great option. The school is yours; we'll figure out a way to get you in and you can do it as an internship. Just apply, okay?'

I had looked at Sahil and he wore a look I couldn't read. Either he was hoping I would display some sense of responsibility or he'd hoped to witness, with much glee, my downfall.

Well, I'd given him plenty of that, hadn't I now?

Riddhi

Weight: I care damn!
Diet Plan: Binge-eating worthy

Plot twist pe plot twist! I know most people say kahaani mein twist but Harsh is broker, so I say plot.

I toh clutched my heart and fell back into my chair. Everyone looked shocked. Total silence. I could only hear ghadi ki tick-tick-tick-tick. Then I realized it's coming from Harsh's stupid pocket watch.

I was toh so shocked I felt like K-serial ki heroine. Not K-drama, K-serial. Big difference. K-drama heroines are gorgeous, confident, successful, in love with chocolatey boys; K-serial heroines were fully bechari, married to boys who couldn't stand up to their Mamas and they wore too much jewellery. Right now, if they made K-serial on Harsh and me, I would be hero and he the heroine because he wore more jewellery than me. But I was so shocked!

The four of them—Mrs Mehta, Sahil Saraogi, Miss Ambika, sorry, Miss Mirambika's 'S' for Saraogi and Shilpa Anand stepped out of the room.

'That's what my brain was trying to tell me!' Giselle said snapping her fingers. 'Mind maps. The name Mira. Somehow, it connects with Ambika. So I had her checked out. We do so many background checks and Ambika S. was yielding no result. But Mira-ambika did.'

I toh didn't know what she was going on about. Or why she was showing her teeth so much to Kainaz and sizzling-hot Varaz Dotwalla. Uff! Wonder what his skincare routine is? Kainaz and Varaz started saying something, but I turned to Jia. She looked white like a Surf Excel ad.

'You looked so happy when you came in. Now what happened?'

'I ... I was happy. But I'm confused now.'

'Yes, yes. You see, Mr Sahil Saraogi is Miss Ambika's brother. But we didn't know that. We also didn't know that Miss Ambika is actually Miss Mirambika—'

'No, I mean how did this even begin?'

'It began with Mrs Mehta coming into the room with all the staff. And then she said—'

'I mean, who complained? How did they get the note? How did Sahil Saraogi get a note? Is there one note or two?'

The four of us turned to each other. Bhai, mudda was the same. We still didn't know.

'I didn't complain,' Kainaz spoke up first. 'Look, Varaz and Mira knew each other many years ago. She's the one who had suggested he try modelling. She'd also told him then that she owns a school, but he'd forgotten about it and, only recently, when she met Varaz did he put two and two together.' Hain? Hain? Hain? Hain? What was she going on about? I ignored her and presented own defence.

'I didn't send email,' I said. 'God swear! Harsh said we have less problems in life, why to make more problems for people?'

Giselle blinked at us. For first time, I stared at her green eyes. They looked so real. Lenses? Really?

'Well, I almost did. In fact, I had a typed-out email sitting in my drafts. And I have to admit, I did think initially that maybe I did send it by mistake after all, but when I checked, it is still in my drafts. And yes, I figured out who she was a couple of days ago too. But I had decided to let it go anyway by then, as discussed with you all.'

I toh took deep, deep breath. Now I understood! 'You mean, you both knew Miss Ambika owns the school? What if we'd complained?'

'But isn't it worse? That she owns the school and this is what she does?' Giselle argued.

'It's all entitlement,' Jia said. 'I didn't complain either, by the way. I've been so caught up in my divorce and Rabia's custody. Which I've got by the way. The paperwork just came in.'

Hai Bhagwan!! Such big news! And now she's telling us!

I toh threw my arms around Jia. Bhaad mein gaya school and Saraogi drama! My Jia was actually smiling! Everyone started congratulating her, and squeezed her hand and all that. So stupid abusive husband had been found after all and he had agreed to sign all papers. The appearance had happened in court and now Rabia was all Jia's.

Before I could ask more detail—vaise only judge's clothes colour I didn't know by now—Mrs Mehta and team were back.

'Sorry about that,' Mrs Mehta said still with very zukaam-wali voice. 'We had to settle something internally.'

'What is the action you'll be taking?' I asked, clutching my heart so that they could all see how I supported Miss Ambika, especially now that she was boss of school and could do good for Syra.

'For starters,' Mrs Mehta said, 'Miss Ambika's services with Champion Valley School will be terminated.'

Immediately, everyone started talking. I didn't know what to say so I just started talking like that only to Harsh.

'But we're not okay with that,' Giselle Savarkar insisted. 'We didn't ask for it.'

'There are many capable teachers who can replace her,' Mrs Mehta reassured us.

'We don't want replacement,' Harsh insisted. 'Syra is very fond of her.'

Again, everyone was talking so the person taking notes went mad only, I think so.

Then, Rajiv Savarkar stood up and Varazji, handsome hunk, joined him, and Mrs Mehta kept trying to get the situation under control but, as I was sitting closest to Miss Ambika, I heard her brother bend down and ask, 'Have you bribed them? How have you managed to get them to stand up for you? They should hate you for what you've said.'

'I'm sorry I said anything about them but they're not standing up for me because I'm Mirambika. They forgave me even before I told them that. They *like* me. They like what I do for their children, for the school!'

'They're only protecting you because they know who you are.'

'It's not true!' I jumped in. Riddhi Makheeja Chhabra always stood up for women. I was not a misogenfem whatever. 'I didn't know who she is till now, Mr Saraogi sir. But she's a good teacher. She should be given second chance!'

Mr Sahil Saraogi looked at me strangely and I think so he spent a minute extra on my golden hairclip but then realized he was looking at Jia sitting behind me. Pata nahin what he was staring at so much. And she at him. I toh looked at her and then at him and then at her, but *Kho Gaye Hum Kahan* was going on.

Finally, Mrs Mehta spoke up. 'Well, seeing that the person who raised the complaint isn't here, maybe it's best if we just postpone the meeting.'

Suddenly my heart stopped beating. What did she mean? Pareetaji had sent email?

Pareeta

Full Term

'We would have gotten here faster, Pareetaji, sorry, Pareeta, not ji, but Kainaz was driving,' Riddhi said breathlessly as they all burst into the hospital room just as I had started to get some shut eye. Riddhi immediately put her generous posterior on my bed.

'And Riddhi was guiding us, instead of putting on Google Maps,' Giselle said without taking her eyes off her phone as she sauntered in, 'so we got even later than expected. She's clearly directionally challenged.'

'Kya matlab?' Riddhi asked offended.

'You said left instead of right and right instead of left.'

'But my hand was showing this way, na? So I meant that side.'

'I'm never criticizing Google Maps again,' Kainaz said.

'And I'm never letting Shivam throw things at drivers again. At least they know my left means right.'

That got me laughing. I was lying in the hospital bed, all wrapped up, exhausted, a drip attached to my arm, having fought the scariest birthing experience ever, and here were my four cartoonish friends the minute I sent them a message. Having a baby in your forties was certainly quite an adventure. But all's well that ends well. The family had been here, she'd been taken to the nursery, the kids had gone down to the cafeteria and, here I was, surrounded by amusing company.

'Put the phone down for once, Giselleji!' Riddhi admonished. 'We're here to see the patient.'

'Stop calling me ji-ji. Makes me feel like an old aunty,' Giselle snapped back.

'But we are all aunties,' I said. 'And look at me. I'm the aunty still having babies!'

Suddenly, they stirred as they realized what they were indeed here for. 'Where is she?'

'In the nursery.'

'Have you thought of a name?' Jia asked.

'Amal.'

They all cooed and then Giselle returned to her phone again. 'I'm so sorry. I've just closed the position for Bathware; hence the email. I'd been looking to hire someone senior for months. You won't believe who accepted the position!'

We all looked at each other blankly.

'Miss Ambika?' Jia asked.

'Ha ha,' Giselle said rolling her eyes. 'No. Mrs Mehta's son. He's a consultant and I got him hired.'

'Mrs Mehta, our principal?' Riddhi asked.

'Yes.'

'Someone said her son lived in Australia.'

'Yes, he was there for an assignment. Now he'll be moving back to India.'

'Achha, Pareetaji, do you know Jia got full custody of Rabia today?'

I was thrilled to hear that. I wrapped my arms around her. Ever since she had told us her story, I felt so personally invested in her fight.

'Please tell me what happened in school,' I asked. 'What was the verdict? Who had sent the email?'

They all turned to me and Giselle raised an eyebrow. 'You did.'

Lesson Fifteen
The Last Bell

From: Grade Coordinator Shilpa Anand <Shilpa.anand@cvs.in>
To: Grade III Parents
Date: 4 March 2023 at 9.00 AM
Sub: Annual Day Performance: Grade III

Dear Parents,

'Enthusiasm is a wealth that is in abundance in childhood' – Sri Sri Ravi Shankar

We are pleased to invite you to our annual day performance by Grade III, which will be held on 10 March 2023 from 9.00 a.m. onwards at the Saraogi Convention Hall.

Please find attached the invite for the same.

Regards,

Shilpa Anand
Coordinator, Grades III, IV & V

Pareeta

3.5 months

I left the baby at home with my mother for the first time, but she wouldn't be too much trouble. Vidya was there, fully capable of handling her, and she loved being the older sister.

'It comes so naturally to me, Mom. Maybe I should have one of my own soon.'

I rolled my eyes and she giggled.

She'd apologized, of course, when she'd confessed that she had accessed my email to send Miss Ambika's note to Mrs Mehta.

'You looked so troubled those days, Mom. I thought it was the note.'

'But you should have asked me before sending out an email impersonating me, Vidya. It caused a lot of trouble.'

She looked torn and embarrassed. 'I've already got a huge lecture from Mrs Mehta and I have apologized to everyone else. But I was worried for you. Especially at the Diwali party. You'd never looked so low.'

'I was. For the first time someone had told me on my face that I was … that I …'

But she's only fifteen. I couldn't tell her how I was indeed trying to save my marriage and it was a shock that someone else could tell so easily.

'You should've talked to me. And I should have talked to you,' I told her instead, giving her a hug.

But that was all in the past now. I was glad we were able to identify who had sent that email to the principal and set the record straight. It was none of us mums. It was my daughter.

The anonymous tip off to Sahil Saraogi was a different matter though.

I had gone to school to withdraw the complaint officially. We all had. Mrs Mehta was not convinced but we'd persisted and she let Miss Ambika off with a warning. It went into her permanent file, of course, but Miss Ambika wasn't really bothered. I guess you didn't have to be when you owned the place and no file could ever be that permanent.

It had been many months since then. How life had changed!

I looked around my room now to ensure that my family had enough of everything before I left for the annual day performance. My mother and daughter were already very hands-on since I had returned to my baking business very soon after. They would be in charge of Amal for the next few hours as we had agreed to meet for coffee right after the annual day performance. All of us fabulous mums. That's what we called the WhatsApp group now. We were no longer normal. We were fabulous! And that felt good!

I slipped into my heels, so thrilled to be wearing them after so many months, got into the car and asked the driver to drop me off at the school auditorium.

There was no way I was going to miss Aryan's end-of-year annual show. A two-hour performance where songs were sung out of tune, dance steps were forgotten, mics were held at shrieking distance and lipstick was applied all over their flaming cheeks. It was always the high point of the academic year.

I noticed Jia already seated in the hall, glowing as she spotted me. I said hello to a few more parents as I walked down the aisle, complimenting Rekha Tandon on her cleverly applied snake-like sindoor, and took a seat next to Jia. She immediately pulled out her phone and showed me pictures of her house.

'Isn't it looking wonderful? Kainaz really has a fabulous sense of design.'

I had to admit it looked beautiful. There were hues of peach and orange, and bright-green pots to add more colour. It was a lighter, understated bohemian look and reflected the change in Jia's emotions, personality and outlook so well.

Jia no longer wore loud make-up. Riddhi had given her a lesson in more is less—imagine that!—and while she covered the scar cleverly, the rest of her face looked naturally beautiful. She was also so radiant because her divorce had finally been settled, she no longer lived in the fear of losing Rabia and she no longer had to divert all her earnings into lawyer fees.

She had also decided to stay on in India and build a home. She'd hired Kainaz to handle the interiors and she was doing a fabulous job refurbishing the place.

There was something else that had changed in Jia's demeanour but I couldn't put a finger on it. She didn't tell us but she smiled a lot more, I noticed. As true friends, we had to give each other space to open up about whatever we wanted, whenever we wanted, if we wanted. Though I did hope she would tell us soon because curiosity was killing me!

'How's the baby?' she asked.

'Like you can expect at this age. Loud!'

We both started to laugh when I felt a hand on my knee.

'Hi.'

'Hi.'

'Sorry I'm late. Couldn't find parking.'

I looked at him, taking in his hazel eyes, his little beard and the lines around his eyes.

'I'm so glad you're here.'

'I've already missed too much,' he said meaningfully.

I tried not to react. I turned to Jia. 'Jia, this is Pankaj.'

She looked surprised. 'Oh ... hi.' They shook hands.

Twenty-two hours after Amal was born, Pankaj had landed up at the hospital, suitcase in hand, a look of resignation on his face. He'd stared at me and I at him. But I hadn't cried.

There were too many cracks to cement in our relationship. Not just the distance—that was the easiest to mend. It was the snapping off of emotions, the unfair division of responsibilities, the casual absenteeism for way too long. We'd spoken about it, gone for therapy and he'd set the wheels in motion to be physically closer to us now. And while he was far more present now than he was earlier, we still had a long way to go.

Giselle

Time: 8.58 a.m.
Unread emails (109)

'What's Kev's role again?' Rajiv asked as we both walked up the stairs to the Saraogi Convention Hall.

'He's some tree or something,' I responded, almost tripping on a step because I was reading through a new project brief that had come my way.

'Does he have lines or …'

'He's talentless, your son. He just has to stand on the stage and sway, I believe.'

'Whenever there's a shortcoming, he becomes *my* son, not *our* son.'

I glared at him and he grinned at me.

'Have you spoken to them?'

'Have I spoken to whom?'

'The mothers.'

'Yes.'

'And they're both coming?'

'Yes.'

'Shit.'

'Shit is right.'

So we decided we wanted to patch things up with our parents. Fifteen years was a very long time. I didn't know where the realization came from—maybe because I saw Pareeta with her mother. What a wonderful relationship they shared, so ever present, so supportive of everything; and I felt a longing for my own. Yes, it hurt my ego to have to ring her while I hoped she could have rung me, especially since Rajiv's mother had called him many years ago and had stayed in touch, but my own, someone who should have understood my choices so much better ... Well, she never had.

It didn't go as well as I'd expected. She was still bitter that I hadn't turned up when my father had been unwell; I blamed her for not being there at all over all these years—but then they'd all come around and now both the mothers were visiting us in Delhi to spend time with Kevin. Kevin who thought his grandparents were dead till now needed a lot of counselling after we announced that they were indeed still alive. Now he kept pestering us to announce that his dead hamster would come to life as well.

We found Jia and Pareeta sitting in the middle wing, holding seats for us, so we waved to them. As we walked towards them, I caught a glimpse of Pankaj. I still thought him a scoundrel for having abandoned Pareeta when she needed him the most, but I had promised to be civil.

As we were walking towards them, surprisingly, I bumped into Dhruv Mehta, Mrs Mehta's son.

'Giselle!' he said.

'Dhruv, how good to see you here!' He looked so different now from his consultant avatar when I'd interacted with him earlier. He was no longer in business suits and crisp shirts. He was wearing jeans and a collared T-shirt, and looked pretty good. We shook hands and I introduced Rajiv.

'Do you come for all the school productions?' I asked curiously.

'Oh no! Not at all. I've just returned from Karamba. That's in Jharkhand, by the way, not a fancy Mexican city that so many people have assumed. I thought I would take the day off.'

'And this is your idea of a day off? Watching three-hundred children make a fool of themselves?'

He laughed.

'The things one must do for being a principal's son!'

He shrugged. 'Actually, my friend Mir ... Ambika, you would know her, she's your son's class teacher, she'd invited me.'

'Oh, is it?'

'Yes. She's leaving, as you may all be knowing,' he said meaningfully.

I nodded. 'I didn't know you were friends.'

'Oh yes, since our school days.'

Yes, I may be wearing coloured contact lenses but my eyes are sharp enough to pick up things unsaid. I nodded and waved.

'Well, we'll see you around then.'

'See you! Oh, and ... er ... I have a position open on my team for a branding specialist. I'll get someone to send it across next week. Please do help.'

'Of course,' I said, always happy to get more business, even if this particular industry was full of shit.

He waved goodbye and I followed Rajiv down the aisle.

Huh! Interesting connection between Miss Ambika and Dhruv Mehta. How had I missed that? I needed to strengthen my mind maps.

Riddhi

Weight: 69.9. 60s! YES!
Diet Plan: Butter chicken. Not given by dietician since I have not paid dietician for a month but that's what I'm eating, I care not!

'Bhaisaheb!' I leaned in, almost bursting with excitement. 'We haven't met. Myself Riddhi Makheeja Chhabra, Pareeta's friend.'

So this was Pankajji! Pareeta's much-spoken-about husband. Thhode se old hain, lekin Pareeta had said they were trying to work things out. It was so difficult to call them Pareeta, Kainaz and Giselle without attaching 'ji' but we were friends now.

'Harsh, this is Pareeta's husband. This is my hubby, Harsh Chhabra.'

'Hello ji. Myself Harsh from Fantasy Homes Realtors.'

'Hi, Harsh. Nice to meet you. Good to meet you too, finally, Riddhi. Pareeta has told me so much about you.'

Hai! Isn't that nice! I know, I know I'm always so famous, but still. I looked at Pareeta and gave her a thumbs up. She gave very small smile. I took the seat next to Jia and she started showing me pictures of the house. Kainaz had done a good job, though the colours were a bit light according to me. Also, there was no chandelier? I suggested the same to her. My Mintu Bhaiya had a showroom in Chandni Chowk which had very nice crystal chandelier. The one in *Om Shanti Om* that fell on Shantipriya? Same to same. We had it in our Rajouri house too. I could get her a discount. Jia didn't look impressed so I told her, dekh le, Jia. If you want to stay in India, you have to have Indian-looking house. Her New York-Shew York style won't work here!

'Thank you for your tip, but I really don't think those ballroom chandeliers will go with my space,' she said.

'Harsh says they're coming back in fashion. Though I don't think so you should take fashion advice from Harsh. Look, even today outfit too loud.'

Okay, I know I was in pink dress with white beads and Harsh kept saying fuchsia-fuchsia but then I told him to keep his Asian Paints acting for his friends because I wasn't going to change!

'I hope so they start on time,' I said. 'I've not had any breakfast. I mean so, I only had oats porridge with chocolate chips—very good it is, Jia, try it—but now I need proper breakfast.'

In a distance, I saw Kainaz and handsome-hunk Varaz walking in. Hai! My heart toh dances like Mithun every time I see him.

'Kannu! Here, here!'

Kainaz didn't hear me so I waved harder. 'Kannu! Kannu! Kainaz! Kainaz!'

She finally saw me and smiled. Some woman came and tried to take seat next to me so I smiled at her. 'Excuse me, this seat is for my friend.' The woman looked angry but theek hai. I quickly patted the seats to show Kainaz I'd reserved them.

So many heads turned when Varazji walked towards our chairs. Hai, to be surrounded by all these good-looking men! And my Harsh dressed in matching Dolce and Gabbana tracksuit. Isse zyada broker type koi ho sakta hai? Phir bhi, he just had facial yesterday so looked good only.

'So excited I am about the performance!' I told Jia. 'What is Rabia doing? Syra is toh singing.'

I then pulled out a big hanky to cry into. When your children perform onstage, you cry. It's the truth of life. Might as well be prepared.

Kainaz

I couldn't believe I had friends who kept a seat for me. And called me Kannu? Um, okay. But it was nice to have friends in a city I had only known for a year. From the city of snobs to my home city.

'Everyone's a snob when they're strangers,' Varaz told me, 'and you felt like a snob to them too. Now look at us. Look at Ahan.'

What an odd year it had been! I had actually started to consider Gurgaon home. We had a two-week break now and I wasn't rushing back to Goa. Even Varaz had looked surprised when I'd said I'd be okay to stay around during term break.

Riddhi immediately grabbed my hand when we reached our seats.

'Is it true? Is it true? Varazji is returning to acting?'

'What? No.'

She looked crestfallen.

'But Syra said Ahaan couldn't come for the playdate because you had magazine people coming over.'

'Yes ... They're coming for me.' I blushed as the others looked at me with interest. 'The Elder Wand, my furniture company, it's getting covered by *Homes and Us*.'

'That's fabulous!' Pareeta said, clapping her hands. They all congratulated me and we had a bit of an embarrassing group hug.

But it was a big deal, really. It wasn't a paid promotion. Some influencer happened to chance upon my workshop and was so impressed with my work that she posted it on her social media. It went viral! And then this magazine had contacted me to do a feature. I had so many orders pending now and even people in the condo now knew me as Kainaz Dotwalla from Elder Wand and not Kainaz Dotwalla, Varaz's wife, which made me feel like the old Kainaz—the one in Goa. Not like I was any less proud of being his wife, but still.

Suddenly, the lights dimmed in the hall, and I saw the others pulling out tissues and handkerchiefs as if ready to cry. As far as I knew, the class was putting up a play on Cinderella but none of it was expected to be *that* tragic. Maybe some things about Delhi and Gurgaon still confused me.

I turned to the stage as the curtains drew and there he stood, Ahaan, in the middle of four other children, ready for the announcement.

'Welcome to the Grade III annual day,' one of the children said. The hall broke out into applause.

'Simi Kukreja's son,' Riddhi leaned forward and whispered to us. 'They live in Magnolias. Very moneyed. We attended their birthday party last year. Too flashy.'

'No judging!' Giselle hissed.

'It's just information!' Riddhi bit back.

'We have …' the other girl on stage began and looked lost.

'Haya Inamdar's daughter. Haya's a theatre personality, no? That's why they keep giving this one roles, but every year she forgets her lines,' Riddhi 'informed' us again.

'No judging!' Giselle said again.

'Sorry, sorry,' Riddhi said.

There was some prompting and then the mic was passed to another child.

'But did you see Rekha Tandon's snake-like sindoor?' Pareeta whispered.

'Oh my god, horrible,' Giselle agreed and everyone nodded.

So much for the no judging rule.

Then it was Ahaan's turn who loudly—a bit too loudly—said, 'Can we request you to please put your phones on silent.'

The sort of things that make your heart swell with pride! The fact that my little boy looked so handsome and spoke so confidently onstage. I felt my eyes sting and now understood why the others were carrying tissue boxes. Promptly Pareeta handed me one.

I wiped my tears as Syra said, 'We would now like to invite Mrs Mehta to light the lamp.'

Riddhi broke out into hysterical sobs.

Jia

> Hi Mom. Rabia missed you at the show.

Sorry beta. But this stupid sprained ankle

> Did the maalish wali come?

Yes. Feeling much better

How did the performance go?

> It was great!

> But she kept saying she wanted Dadi to come

I'll definitely come next time

Are you heading to office now?

> In a bit

Where are you?

> At a coffee shop

> Mom. I don't say this enough. Thank you.

> For what?

> For what you do for me. For being with me and Rabia. For having left everything for us.

> I am here for as long as you need me

> I'll never stop needing you Mom

> Very few women want to live with their mothers in law!

> They don't have the one I have.

> I know it took a lot for you to support me Mom

> You're like Mother India. You took my side instead of your son's

> I took the side of the one who was right

> I'm sorry for what he did to you

> Me too

> I can leave if you want me to, Jia

> I never want you to leave, Mom.

> You are my family

> Even when my own left me

> Wait, why are we doing this on messages?

> I'm just getting done with coffee with the ladies. Can I call?

> Hi Jia. This is Sahil. It was good to see you at school the other day.

> Would you like to catch up for a cup of coffee some time?

Ambika

'What will you have?' Dodo asked me as we stood at the Starbucks counter.

'Cappuccino. You?'

'I'll take a grande Americano.'

I rolled my eyes. 'So firang, Dodo.'

'I'll get it,' he said taking out his wallet.

'No. I have enough dough for a coffee now, thank you.'

'You'll have more than enough for a coffee now that you've completed your year, *Ambika*!' he teased. 'But let me get this. One Cappuccino, tall, and one Americano, grande, please.'

'And your name is?' the cashier asked.

'Dhruv. Thanks.'

'So I saw you met Giselle Savarkar,' I said as we walked over to an empty table.

'You were keeping an eye on me from the wings, is it?'

'You know me. I'm territorial.'

'We have her to thank for bringing me back to India.'

'Why is that a blessing?'

'Because that way I get to be close to you.'

I rolled my eyes. 'What did you think of the performance?'

'So bad!'

'Wasn't it? I thought so too.'
'Though Mrs Mehta looked quite pleased.'
'You're so weird, calling your own mum Mrs Mehta.'
'You're so weird calling your brother fuck face.'
'Okay, so we all have dysfunctional families.'

The cashier called his name so we dropped the topic and Dodo went across to fetch it. When he returned with our coffee, he sat down and said, 'She's pretty.'

I turned to look at the cashier, who was, at best, average looking. 'Okay, I guess.'

'Not the cashier. I meant Giselle. She must've been a looker at some point.'

'She must be in her forties, Dodo. You make her sound like she's eighty!'

He nodded. 'Yeah, but you know, age starts showing up when you have kids. Look at you. Thirty kids around you and look how you've aged in the last one year.'

I whacked him. 'I have not!'

'You totally have! You haven't let out one expletive all morning, you haven't cribbed about having to stand in line back there and you actually called me Dhruv once.'

'That's your name, isn't it?'

'Yes, but I can't remember the last time you used it.'

'That's because you've always been a Dodo since you sneaked into the girls' hostel with that love note.'

'Did you see how green you'd become when you read the love note? I still remember what I said:
If you can dream—and not make dreams your master
If you can think—and not make thoughts your aim;
I can't do any of it, Mira Saraogi
Because without you I am in pain.

I started to laugh but I remembered it word for word too. So I joined him.

Your smile lights up my life
Your laughter makes me insane
Tell me truthfully, Mira Saraogi
Tell me if you feel the same.

I punched his arm playfully. 'Wordsworth will be turning in his grave right now.'

'It's Rudyard Kipling. And I'm still waiting for an answer.'

'Well, now I remember what I said. I said I cannot be seeing my maths teacher's son so it's a hard no!'

'What's your answer now? She's no longer your maths teacher!'

'She's my employer!'

'She's your *ex*-employer.'

'No. She may still be my employer.'

'Wait, what?'

'It means I may go back to Champion Valley School.'

'Are you serious?'

'Yes. Obviously I can't go back as a teacher. I know that was just an understanding to let me have that job without any credentials.'

He looked at me incredulously. 'Mira, you were the school topper, top of your class for as long as you studied in uni—'

'Yes, but I didn't finish anything! I don't have a teaching degree.'

'Do you want a teaching degree?'

'No. I don't think so. I mean, it was a sweet experience. I may hate children a little less now. But I don't mind this whole school set up really. Anyway, keeping with the theme of the year, I forgive her.'

'Who? Mrs Mehta?'

'Not your mum. I mean Miss Sahiba, the squealer!'

'She's been retained?'

'Yes.'

So the deal was this. During the proceedings where Mrs Mehta, Dodo's mum, my former high school teacher, my current employer—one woman, many roles in my life—insisted that they take action against me, the mothers retracted their complaint and said I seemed to be doing a decent job of keeping their kids engaged in school. So all was forgotten and life returned to normal.

But later, when my identity became public knowledge, thanks to so many people being privy to the meeting, Miss Sahiba, the other section's teacher, who lived with the fairies, had confessed to Mrs Mehta that it was she who had sent the note to Sahil. She had apparently been appalled by how lax I had been with the class and how much I was getting away with all the time because Shilpa Anand would often bring her in to showcase the good and bad practices of teaching. She wanted to ensure the reputation of the school didn't suffer on my account.

Even though she was horrified at my general behaviour always, the last straw had been the parents report card that she had discovered on my table a day before the PTM. And she had photographed it and kept it to showcase directly to Mrs Mehta. Then, on the day of the PTM, when I'd dropped all the papers upon seeing Riddhi's ridiculous outfit, and when Shilpa and Sahiba had come to help me pick them up, she saw it as an opportunity to slip it into one of the report cards, hoping one of the parents would complain. But when nobody did, she decided to take things into her own hands and escalate it to Sahil, as a well-wisher and CVS loyalist.

And the rest, of course, is history.

Why had she confessed? We have no idea. Perhaps she just didn't want to get into trouble now that she knew who I was. Or perhaps she knew someone else would be in trouble because I certainly wasn't. Whatever it was, I decided to let her be. After all, I did appreciate the fact that she was so dedicated to the school and actually cared about the quality of teaching staff.

That's when I'd felt the first jolt too. That I thought of the school as my own. I felt responsible for it.

So many little things started to make sense then. The values, the way we spoke to the parents, our ethos, the feeling of being one big family. I actually started enjoying the training sessions, I saw merit in the quotes we put at the beginning of our emails, I started paying more attention to the plight of parents. I was far kinder in my interactions with them, far more helpful, far more involved, a whole lot more patient.

And that's when I decided that I wanted to remain a part of Champion Valley School. Not in teaching capacity but as something else. I didn't know what right now. Maybe in their admin team. Maybe in their marketing team. Maybe in their—

'Hey, isn't that Sahil?' Dodo lowered his voice.

I looked up and saw Sahil enter the café with a very familiar-looking woman. Curly haired, curvaceous, evident scar on her cheek, bright-eyed. Instantly I placed her. Rabia's mum, Jia. They took a table at the other end of the café and looked pretty engrossed in each other.

'Looks like there's a love story brewing there,' Dodo said leaning in. 'How about we start one of our own?'

I kicked him under the table. 'Fuck off, Dodo!'

He sighed. 'I'll wait, Mirambika Saraogi. I'll keep waiting.'

I saw the way they held each other's eye as they spoke, the tenderness that showed on his face, the way his leg started to bounce in nervousness and my heart went out to him. I automatically started rooting for him. Because that's what family felt like. And I wanted mine back.

Acknowledgements

The acknowledgements section of *this* book is really the most important because it's a disclaimer that neither the school, the teachers nor the mums in this book are specific to anyone I know! It's all a figment of my imagination—albeit *inspired* by so many of you! I also want to state that the purpose of the book was not to provide social commentary and critique, but a little bit of drama and a lot of comic relief that we seem to miss in our lives every so often.

Now with that out of the way, I want to first thank Swati Daftuar, my erstwhile editor, for accepting the manuscript with much enthusiasm, as she always does, and seeing potential in the storyline. And a special thanks to my current editor, Rashmi Menon, for refining it and sending me much needed love and encouragement along the way. Thank you, Poulomi Chatterjee, Arcopol Chaudhuri and the rest of the HarperCollins India team for showing your faith in my writing once again. And thank you, Shreya Mukherjee, for your fabulous editing. Like I said earlier, you guys make dreams come true.

In the true Academy-award style, I also want to thank my family—Moksh, Zayn and Iram for allowing me to stay lost in the characters and giving me space to write them. Thank you, Mum, Aapa, J, Kyrah, Mum-in-law, Dad-in-law, Nas and Aye, for your constant support and pride in what I do. Thank you for pitching in, cheering me on and believing in me, always. Also a big shout out to my husband's mother's brother's daughters—this one's for the aunties! :D

Thank you to everyone who has picked up my earlier books and taken out the time to write to me, to tell me I made you laugh and for nudging me to write my next. Please keep them coming! I hope to write the next one sooner as promised.

And last but not the least, thank you, all my mommy friends—friends who became moms, moms who became friends, friends who remained friends through thick and thin (you know who you are!)—for peppering my life with your funny stories every day and helping me whip up new characters every time.

It was, as always, great fun writing this book, even though I went through a bit of a personality split by having to step into different shoes and hearing different voices in my head all the time. But I am rather pleased with how the mums and the teachers have taken shape and I hope you've enjoyed reading their journeys as much as I've enjoyed writing them.

About the Author

Zarreen Khan is a Delhi-based author, who quit her marketing job to pursue her passion for writing. Her books, *I Quit! Now What?*, *Koi Good News?* and *My Best Friend's Son's Wedding* have been widely appreciated and sold for movie rights.

You can reach her @zarreenk on Instagram.

HarperCollins *Publishers* India

At HarperCollins India, we believe in telling the best stories and finding the widest readership for our books in every format possible. We started publishing in 1992; a great deal has changed since then, but what has remained constant is the passion with which our authors write their books, the love with which readers receive them, and the sheer joy and excitement that we as publishers feel in being a part of the publishing process.

Over the years, we've had the pleasure of publishing some of the finest writing from the subcontinent and around the world, including several award-winning titles and some of the biggest bestsellers in India's publishing history. But nothing has meant more to us than the fact that millions of people have read the books we published, and that somewhere, a book of ours might have made a difference.

As we look to the future, we go back to that one word— a word which has been a driving force for us all these years.

Read.